MICHELLE LYNN ROSS

Back To You

A Fawn Creek Christmas Novella

FAWN
CREEK
PRESS

To my readers, who make my little town of Fawn Creek feel more real every day.

Acknowledgments

This book would not have been possible without the support of so many incredible people. But, I want to give a special thank you to Dala, Christian and Billie for being my ARC readers and helping me polish this story so it could truly shine.

Thank you to my husband for patiently listening to me brainstorm at all hours and to my kids for understanding when dinner ran a little late because I was finishing up one more scene. Your love and support makes every story possible.

And of course, thank you to my readers, who make writing about Fawn Creek such a joy. Your encouragement, laughter, and belief in my stories inspire me every day.

I hope you enjoy Reagan and Cash's story as much as I do.

Chapter 1

"How did we end up with this much crap?" I grumble aloud to no one in particular as I sit in the middle of my dining room floor surrounded by moving boxes. "It's going to take me until the new year to get all of this sorted through." Giving up, I toss a wadded ball of butcher paper towards the kitchen and lay down on the carpet.

"Mom, we're out of milk." My son, Nolan, reports as he sticks his head out of the swinging door that divides the dining room from the kitchen. He holds up the empty milk jug as evidence, interrupting my mini meltdown.

I groan, still not removing my eyes from the ceiling fan above me. "I'll go to the store in the morning."

"Mooooom. I'm hungry. I wanted to have cereal for dinner," Nolan whines.

"Isn't that what you've had for the past two days? Can't you maybe have some leftover turkey that Grandma sent home? Or leftover tacos from last night? You do know that we have other food, right? You don't have to eat cereal. And protein is actually good for you."

Nolan lets out a heavy sigh. "Mom please? I already dumped the cereal into a bowl. I was really looking forward to it."

I sit up, exasperated. "Fine. Keep an eye on Maisie while I'm gone."

"Can't she keep an eye on herself?" He retorts. "Or can you have Sadie do it? I'm in the middle of a game."

"First off, Sadie is upstairs reading," I say, pointing towards the staircase leading up to my sixteen-year-old daughter's bedroom. "And secondly, no, Maisie cannot watch herself. She is nine. It's not like you actually have to do anything. She's lying in her bed watching a movie, not bothering anyone. Just make sure she doesn't cook anything or use power tools."

Nolan rolls his eyes, and I turn to him with a stern expression on my face.

"Do you want milk or not? I'll happily go back to unpacking, and you can have water in your cereal instead."

"Gross," my teenage son says as he scrunches his nose. "Fine. I'll watch her."

"How kind of you." I grumble as I stand from the floor and glance at my reflection in the entryway mirror. I've been wearing the same clothes since crawling out of bed this morning. My comfiest pair of flannel pajama pants and a stained gray sweatshirt that proclaims: *Fawn Creek Prairie Dogs. Established 1881.*

I adjust my messy bun and shrug. Sure, I probably should change into something more presentable. But it's almost 8:30 at night. The store will be closing soon, and I likely won't see anyone other than a bored teenager running the cash register. That's the last person I'm worried about seeing me.

I slip on my sneakers and grab my purse. "I'll be back in fifteen minutes with your milk." I call out to Nolan, who has already retreated up the stairs to his bedroom to continue his video game.

"Man, it's nice to be appreciated around here." I mumble

under my breath before stepping out into the cool autumn evening.

It's the weekend following Thanksgiving, and my hometown of Fawn Creek, Kansas, is experiencing its first cold front of the season. I wasn't ready for the cold, especially after living in Houston for the last ten years. It's a shock to the system, to say the least. But life and seasons change, don't they?

A year ago, I would have told you I'd never move back to my hometown. Truthfully, I loved Houston. We all loved being close to the Gulf. I loved the kids' school district and being a stay at home mom. I especially loved my husband, Mark. He worked hard to provide for our family. And I thought he loved me, too. But, apparently, he loved railing his twenty-five-year-old assistant on his desk even more. So, to say that it was a surprise when he handed me divorce papers last spring is a bit of an understatement. He basically handed me the papers while he was packing his things to move in with his cute little assistant-turned-girlfriend, Brittani.

Even with the divorce looming over my head, I would have stayed in Houston forever, honestly. But Mark wanted to sell the house and split the profit, and he had that written into our divorce agreement. There's no way I could have bought anything comparable to the mini mansion that my kids were raised in. At least not in our school district. So, once the house finally sold, I took my half of the profit and bought a new place in my hometown instead.

Luckily, I was able to find a cute, two-story, four-bedroom house with a wraparound porch and a white picket fence, just blocks away from my parents' house. As a bonus, it's within walking distance of both schools. So, with the kids' consent and just a little grumbling, we made the 600-mile move back to my

3

hometown to start all over again. Hopefully, I won't regret it.

I turn the corner off Main Street, and the Fawn Creek Market comes into view. The glow of the neon open sign shines brightly just above the one and only vehicle parked in the lot. It's a tan four-door sedan with a missing front bumper and a primer-colored fender. Hopefully, this indicates that it is the car of a teenager. One that is likely hiding behind the register staring at their phone, too worried about TikTok to worry about some crazy middle-aged lady in her messy bun and pajama pants buying a gallon of milk. *Thank God.* I never would have gone to the store in Houston looking like this. Even if I was sick, I did my hair and makeup and put on at least a matching workout set before walking out the door. But, here? In Fawn Creek? I'm a new person. Or maybe I'm just turning back into the version of me that I was before I left here. Either way, I think I like it.

I step through the automatic door, and the teen boy behind the counter barely moves his head to acknowledge me. He nods, and I nod in return, as though it's some secret agreement that neither of us wants to be here. Without further pause, I make a beeline for the dairy aisle, quickly locating a gallon of 2% milk, before something else catches my eye. A sale on my favorite snack. Buttery movie theater popcorn.

After all the unpacking I've been doing today, I deserve a treat. I grab a box and then make a beeline for the only acceptable snack companion: dill pickle spears.

I pause in the aisle as my eyes glaze over the multitude of choices, finally finding the jar I'm looking for on the bottom shelf. And, lucky for me, it's the last one. I squat down, balancing the milk and popcorn against my knee to grab the jar and finally complete this errand. I've just gotten back to standing when a voice from my past interrupts me.

"Well, look who it is, Reagan Miller in the flesh."

That voice is all it takes for me to forget where I am and how to hold things, or really any other thing that's happened in my world for the last seventeen years.

The jar of pickles slips from my hand and crashes to the floor, resulting in a spray of pickle juice and shards of glass all around me. The liquid quickly soaks my shoes and flannel pajama pants, snapping me back to reality.

"Dammit," I squeal, jumping back from the mess.

Of course, he would be the one to witness this.

Cash Hartwell. My first love and my first heartbreak.

Immediately, I crouch down, reaching for the nearest shard of glass, but a hand closes gently around my wrist. I look up to find his eyes meeting mine. His face is just inches from my own, creating a flutter in my stomach that can only be caused by this man.

"Don't," he says, low and firm. "Dillon will get it. You are going to cut yourself."

I glance up, and sure enough, the teenage cashier is already shuffling towards us, broom and dustpan in hand. His expression makes it clear that he is just as horrified as I am about my pickle mess.

Sorry, kid. So much for an easy, boring night at the grocery store.

I nod and stand, stepping back, allowing the boy to do his job, apologizing profusely to the cashier while slowly releasing my wrist from Cash's grip.

"Are you okay? You're not cut or hurt, are you?" Cash asks, examining me from inches away.

I shake my head. "No. I'm okay."

Satisfied with my answer, he smirks. "I see your snacking habits haven't changed since I last saw you," he says, motioning

5

towards the popcorn still clutched under my arm.

"You remember I like to eat popcorn and pickles?"

He scoffs. "Remember? I'm the one who taught you. The addition of milk is a weird touch though."

I let out a soft chuckle and shake my head. "The milk is for Nolan, my son."

His eyebrows soften. "You have a kid. Of course, you do. I knew that."

I pause, biting my lip. "I have three. Two girls and a boy. In fact, I should probably get back home to them," I say, turning my head to glance towards the front of the store, as Dillon finishes sweeping up my mess.

"Don't forget your pickles," Cash reminds me with a grin.

I frown, looking down at the dustpan full of my evening snack. "That was the last jar. I guess it just wasn't meant to be." Even as the words leave my mouth, I know that I'm talking about something much deeper than pickles. "Well, I'd better get going. I'll see you around." With that, I turn on my heel, clutching my popcorn and milk, and follow Dillon to the front of the store, leaving Cash Hartwell where he belongs, behind me.

Chapter 2

After a sleepless night of lying in bed, reminiscing about my complicated past with Cash, morning comes much too soon. In fact, it seems that just as I finally start to fall into a deep REM cycle, my phone buzzes with an incoming call from my mother. I reach over in my dimly lit bedroom and retrieve the device, hitting the answer button.

"Hello?"

"Reagan? Are you awake? You're coming to church today, aren't you?" My mother asks, her voice oozes with hope and concern.

"Yes, I'm up. I've been up for hours." I lie, attempting to hide the exhaustion in my voice. Surely God gives extra grace for Sunday morning fibs, doesn't He? "What time is church again?"

"9:30."

I pull the phone from my ear and check the time. It's nine o'clock on the dot. It's going to take a genuine miracle in order for the four of us to get ready and into a church pew on time. But we have to make it happen, if not for us, for my mother.

Ever since the day Mark filed for divorce, both of my parents have been nothing less than supportive. As soon as I called with the news, Mom got on a plane and came to stay with us, leaving behind her own life and responsibilities to help me with mine. She took care of the kids and the house and, most of all, me. She saw what was needed and took care of it all. This allowed me the time I needed to grieve my marriage and the life that I thought I'd have until the day I died. The least I can do is get my butt out of bed and sit next to her on Sunday morning.

"We will be there. Save us a seat." I promise, swinging my legs over the side of my bed and landing my feet on the floor.

"Perfect. We will see you then." She answers, her voice full of optimism.

"See you soon. Love you."

Without a second to waste, I toss my phone on the bed and make my way into the hall to wake my children. First, I knock and then stick my head in Sadie's room.

"Hey, Sadie," I say, just above a whisper. "You need to get up, Sis. We have thirty minutes to get to church."

Sadie grumbles in response before pulling her blanket over her head.

"For real. Get up, please," I plead.

"Fine," She mumbles in response, followed by a loud sigh.

I thank her and close her door before moving down the hall. I knock on Nolan's door, and then stick my head inside the room after he fails to respond. "Nolan, time to get up for church. We're running late."

Nolan opens just one eye to glance at me. "Mom. Can't I just sleep in? I'm tired."

"No, bro. I warned you guys yesterday that we were going to church today. We have less than half an hour. We have to get up now."

Nolan sits up in his bed and turns to face me, his expression full of disgust. "Did you just bro me?"

"Yes, bro. Now, get moving." I grin, despite myself. "We're leaving in twenty minutes."

Next up, Maisie. Her door is already open, and somehow she is sleeping sideways on her twin-size bed with her legs dangling off the edge. "Maze..." I say, making my way towards her, gently patting her back. "Hey, time to get up for church."

Her eyes spring open immediately. "Church!" She exclaims, flying out of her bed and running towards her closet, nearly knocking me over in the process.

"We have to kind of hurry. I might have overslept." I admit.

"That's okay! I can be fast. You go get ready, too. Don't worry about me. I'm a big girl."

Following my daughter's instructions, I nod and turn to march back towards my room. I proceed to my closet and dig through the boxes of clothes that I haven't yet even begun to unpack. The only choice I have at this point is to dump it all onto my bed and deal with the aftermath later. I can't believe I didn't think to unpack a dress, or at least something church-appropriate, yesterday during all my sorting.

"Mom, do I have to go to church?" A teenage voice interrupts me as I add to the giant clothing pile on my bed.

I turn to face Sadie with a raised brow. She's still wearing her T-shirt and flannel sleep pants from last night. "Yes, Sadie, you do."

"Why?" she groans.

"Because I want you to. And because it's important to your grandmother. Besides, it's a good way to get plugged in with other kids in this brand new town." I offer, although the look on Sadie's face tells me that all my reasons have fallen short. "Why don't you want to go?"

Sadie sits on my bed with a huff. "Well, for one thing. My

hair looks stupid," she says, running her fingers through her springy curls. "And I have nothing to wear. Plus, my room isn't unpacked yet. I have so much to do, and it's just making me even more anxious about school tomorrow."

I locate my missing dress and hold it up to examine how wrinkled it is. Nothing a dryer and a wet dishtowel can't fix, if I hurry. Then, I turn and take a seat next to my daughter on my bed.

"Sadie, I know this moving and starting all over thing has been hard, especially during your junior year of high school. I get it, and I'm sorry. But starting over in a new place can be fun. Maybe if you go today you can meet someone. Even just one familiar face at school tomorrow will make your first day easier. Trust me."

Sadie rolls her eyes. "Fine, but it's just church, right? Not Sunday school and a basement potluck afterwards?"

I laugh. "Just church. Then we can use the excuse that we need to get home and unpack before you guys start school tomorrow."

Sadie lets out a deep sigh before shrugging in agreement. "Okay. I'll go get ready then."

I pull her into a hug. "Thank you. I promise you, this town really is pretty great. I can't wait for you to see it."

* * *

"Nice work, everyone. Ready and out the door with thirty seconds to spare." I say, handing each child a granola bar as I pick up my purse and usher them towards the door. If we go now, we can get there and get seated without the entire sanctuary watching us walk in.

I fling open the door and look down to see a mason jar on the porch below. I pick the jar up to examine it and find a folded-up note underneath.

This is way better than that store-bought crap, anyway.
  -C

I turn the jar in my hand, examining the contents. Homemade pickles. Not just any homemade pickles, but Cash's mom's. Holding the jar in my hand causes a rush of memories to come flooding back. Every Saturday, that woman used to send me home with a jar of these and a loaf of homemade bread without fail.

She used to joke about having a pickle bar at mine and Cash's wedding one day and said that she was already stocking up in cabinets to prepare for it. But, those days seem like they were from a lifetime ago.

I wonder if she even knows I have these. Would she approve? Does she hate me for breaking her son's heart and leaving town? For going to college and not turning back? Unfortunately, I'm sure I'm only minutes away from finding out. Undoubtedly, she will be at church today, too.

"Mom! I thought we were running late!" Sadie calls to me from her open car door in the driveway. "Are we going or not?"

I glance down at the jar once more before slipping it into my bag. "Yes, I'm coming. Sorry."

Let's go face this town.

* * *

With a deep breath, I swing the old wooden door to the Methodist

11

church open and step inside the sanctuary, searching for my mother. It's not long before her light blue floral dress catches my eye. She's seated next to my dad, with her Bible open in her lap, already lost in the word before service starts.

"Follow me." I whisper to my children. We got this far this morning with no small-town reunions, and if I timed it right, like I hope I did, we should be able to grab a seat just as Pastor DeWitt takes the stage to share the morning announcements. At least this will save us from small talk until the service is over. Unfortunately, though, I seem to have forgotten just how persistent small-town small talk really is.

"Reagan Miller, is that you?" A familiar soft voice rings through the air and stops me in my tracks.

So close.

I grit my teeth and turn to face Sharon Hartwell, Cash's mom. Before I can even speak, she pulls me into a tight hug. Her familiar scent of flour and cinnamon, no doubt from baking homemade cinnamon rolls before church this morning, reaches my nose and transports me back twenty years. Back to when I was just a seventeen-year-old girl that knew it all, at least as far as I was concerned. The girl who was head over heels in love with this woman's son. The man I was sure I was going to spend my life with.

Sharon releases me, but only to take a step back and give me a once-over. I suppose the concern I had over whether she is still mad at me after all these years was useless worrying.

"Reagan, you haven't aged a bit," she whispers before turning to look at my kids standing next to me. "Are these your children?"

I nod and point to each of my kids, introducing them to Sharon, one by one, ending with Maisie.

Sharon smiles softly and bends down to look at my sweet girl. "Maisie, would you like to come to children's church with me?" She offers. "It's a lot more fun than listening to old Pastor DeWitt ramble on."

Maisie nods excitedly before turning to me. "Is it okay, Mama?" She pleads.

"Yes, of course. Sharon, do I need to come fill out paperwork or sign her in?"

Sharon looks at me bewildered. "To go to church? No, you don't need paperwork to go to church. You were in the city for too long, girl. Maisie, do you have any allergies?"

"Nope!" My daughter answers cheerily.

"Good enough for me. Let's go." Sharon declares, pointing Maisie towards the hallway to go to her classroom. "Mom, you can pick her up in her classroom after service, just down the hall."

"Okay," I agree as I watch them disappear down the hall before turning to realize that my other children have since abandoned me. They are seated next to my parents, both fixated on their cellphones, waiting for the service to start. Quickly, I make my way to join them, just as the pastor takes his place on stage.

This morning went better than expected, that's for sure. I expected nothing short of a disaster. But instead, I was met with a hug, homemade pickles and a kiddo excited for Sunday school. Maybe everything will be just fine.

Chapter 3

"Okay. I'm going to go grab your sister, and I'll meet you guys at the car," I tell Sadie, handing over my car keys. "You can start it, just don't drive off and leave me, please."

Sadie rolls her eyes and takes the keys. "Like I would ever do that. Nolan, on the other hand..."

"Oh, believe me. I know. Don't let your brother try anything crazy either."

Sadie nods before gathering my keys and leading her brother to the car. I watch as my textbook oldest child and even more textbook middle child disappear into the parking lot before moving to retrieve Maisie.

Carefully, I make my way down the crowded hallway of classrooms, avoiding rubbing against colorful children's artwork that adorns the walls. I peek my head into the room that's labeled for third-grade students and smile as Maisie and I make eye contact. She makes a mad dash for the door, eyes lit up with excitement.

"Mom! There you are! Can I please be in the Christmas play?" Maisie begs, jumping up and down excitedly.

"Um. What Christmas play?" I ask, my mind already racing with possible questions. How much of my time will this take? When is practice? What if she tries out and doesn't get a part?

She'll be crushed during a time when she's experienced so much heartbreak already.

"I don't know. Mrs. Sharon can tell you all about it. She said that I would be very good at it," Maisie reports excitedly. "Please, Mom?"

I slowly nod, taking in the information. "Maybe, Maisie. Let's talk about it when we get home, okay? Your brother and sister are waiting in the car."

Maisie lets out a heavy huff. "Fine."

"Did you have fun in class?" I ask, turning to lead her towards the door of the church, hoping to change the subject for a few minutes.

"Yes. It was so much fun. I can't wait to come back next week. Plus, I made two new friends who are in my grade. Hopefully, they will be in my class. And I just really want to do the play. It's my dream, Mom."

So much for changing the subject.

"Reagan! Maisie!" Sharon's voice calls down the hall. I spin my heel to face her, as she quickens her steps to reach us. "I'll see you girls next week, okay? And Maisie, if you want to do the play, just come to Children's Church on Wednesday at 6:30." Sharon moves her eyes to meet mine. "That's quite a girl you have there, Reagan. She reminds me so much of you when you were little. She's a lot of fun, and we would love to have her in the Christmas play."

"Mrs. Sharon's the director." Maisie informs me.

Sharon continues. "The performance will be during service on the Sunday before Christmas. We will practice on Wednesday nights. And if you need help getting her here for practice because of work or whatever, you just let me know." She says, handing me a slip of paper with her phone number on it. "I know being a single mom can be hard, and I'm happy to help as much as I can."

I nod and take the paper, examining it closely. "You changed your number."

Sharon chuckles. "Oh, honey, that's just my cell phone number. The house phone is still the same. I'm probably the last one in town to have a landline, but Rick insists we keep it. He is adamant that if one of the kids needs us, they will at least remember the home phone number."

"He's not wrong. I think I know your home number better than I know my social security number." I laugh. "Even after all these years."

Sharon chuckles. "Well, there for a while you were calling our house just about every day. I meant what I said, Reagan. Not only for the play. If you ever need help, call me. If you can't get off work in time to get Maisie, or if you need help... I'm here for you."

I nod. "Thank you. I really appreciate it. But work isn't going to be a concern for me just yet. I started looking as soon as I put in an offer on my house, but I haven't found anything yet. It's hard to find a job in a small town."

"The school is always looking for substitute teachers." She offers with a shrug. "That might be worth checking into. Then, you'll only work while the kids are in school."

"That's a good idea. I'll look into that. Even if it's just something to get me by for now." I say, looking down at Maisie. "Well, I think we'd better head home. The other two are waiting in the car, and we still have a lot of unpacking to do. They are going back to school tomorrow, so it's going to be a busy week."

We exchange our goodbyes and within minutes Maisie and I are making our way across the parking lot to my SUV. I'm almost to the driver's side door when I turn and see a familiar Fawn Creek resident climbing onto his motorcycle. I turn on my heel and walk towards Cash.

"Morning," I say as I close the distance between us.

Upon seeing me, he sends me that familiar smoldering smirk that used to cause me to melt into a puddle as a teenage girl. Admittedly, that hasn't changed a bit since we were young.

"Morning. Did you get my delivery?"

"I did. How'd you know where I live?" I ask, crossing my arms in front of my chest and raising a brow.

He shrugs. "It's Fawn Creek. When a house sells around here, word travels pretty fast."

"Right." I nod in acknowledgment, glancing at the motorcycle he's sitting on, with his helmet in his lap. "Is this the same bike you had when we were kids?"

He pats the side as though he's petting the machine. "This is the one."

"I can't believe you've kept it for all these years."

"Well, when you find something good, you hang on to it. I learned that a long time ago." He counters, staring back at me with those piercing green eyes. The eyes I used to find myself constantly lost in all those years ago.

I have a feeling he's not just talking about his motorcycle.

HONK!

The sound of the horn of my Tahoe rings through the parking lot and startles me, causing me to jump just a little bit. I turn to look at my car, where all three of my children are staring back, motioning for me to hurry up.

"I guess I'd better get going." I say. "Thanks for the pickles."

"Anytime. See ya, Rae." Cash answers as he slides on his motorcycle helmet.

17

I climb into the car and close the door, watching him drive away before putting on my seat belt.

"Who was that?" Sadie asks, raising a brow.

I shake my head. "Just a friend from high school."

"He did not look like just a friend," Sadie replies.

"And he has a motorcycle. Do you think he will let me drive it since he's your friend?" Nolan asks.

"Absolutely not." I answer almost before Nolan can finish asking the question.

"Dang it." Nolan grumbles in reply.

I put the car in drive and begin our journey home, still reeling from the last twenty-four hours and my two run-ins with Cash. I knew I'd see him again at some point. It was a given when I decided to move back home, but I didn't expect it to happen so quickly.

"Mom. I have five reasons you should let me do the Christmas play. Are you ready?" Maisie asks, interrupting my thoughts.

"Like we have any choice other than listening." Nolan murmurs.

Maisie clears her throat, ignoring her brother. "One. The play is at church, and it's about Jesus' birthday, and that's super important. Two. It's my dream to be in a play, so this would literally be my dream come true."

Nolan groans in the backseat. "Your dream? Since when?"

"Since today." She retorts. "Three. Mrs. Sharon is the director, and she said I would be really good. She even said that I was fun, and you said being fun is a good thing."

I raise an eyebrow and glance at Maisie in the rearview mirror, but don't interrupt her speech.

"Four. I don't like to play sports and we can't sign up for dance class until after Christmas, so this would give me something

18

else to be awesome at."

Maisie then leans forward dramatically to finish delivering her final point. "And five. When I become a famous actress and I win an Oscar, I will totally thank you in my speech. Like: 'This is for my mom, who let me be the sheep in the church Christmas play'."

Nolan can't help himself and bursts into laughter. "A sheep? That's what you want to be?"

Maisie shrugs. "Well, I don't know what the parts are yet! Maybe it's a cool sheep. A lead sheep. A sheep that saves Christmas."

I pull the Tahoe into the driveway before turning to look back at Maisie. She is sitting in the second row, behind the passenger seat. Her hands are clasped in prayer position, and her bottom lip is sticking out. I have to hand it to her; she has that begging puppy-dog expression down.

"Please, Mom? You don't even have to get me a Christmas gift this year. This is all I want."

I let out a heavy sigh. "Okay, Maisie. You may be in the Christmas play, but you have to put in the work. That means studying your lines without being asked."

"I promise, Mom!" Maisie squeals. "This is going to be the best Christmas ever!"

"I hope you're right." I mumble to myself as I open the car door and follow an excited Maisie into the house, with Sadie and Nolan trailing behind.

Once I've eaten a turkey sandwich for lunch, finishing up the leftovers my mom sent home with me, it's time to get back to the mission at hand; unpacking this house so I can make it feel more like home. Honestly, when we closed on the house last Tuesday, I assumed that all the unpacking and settling would be

19

done by now. In fact, I had big plans to spend the day wrapped in a blanket while slowly sipping a mug of coffee in order to prepare myself for the kids going to school tomorrow. Sadly, between Thanksgiving with my family and church and just the general feelings of sadness that I'm still experiencing following my divorce, things are taking longer than I expected. Instead, I worked hard to get the kids' rooms unpacked, hoping to give them at least some feeling of normalcy. At least I managed to accomplish that, with their help.

Now, I just have to deal with the rest of the house. And the sooner I get done, the sooner I can begin to really feel settled into Fawn Creek.

I make my way towards the pile of boxes in the corner of the kitchen and select one labeled *Coffee Cups*.

I use a kitchen knife to cut through the clear packing tape before removing the first item from the box. After unwrapping the butcher paper, I uncover a coffee mug Sadie gave me for Mother's Day two years ago that proclaims *World's Okayest Mom*. Next, I uncover a handmade mug that I picked up from a little shop in Orange Beach, Alabama. I remember how excited I was to find a mug with a cut out to keep my hands warm while I sip my tea. Even if it never got cold enough in Houston to really need it, I'll definitely need it this winter.

I sigh and place the mug on the counter, fighting back tears as I realize how hard this Christmas will be not only for myself but for the kids, too. We all have a lot of adjusting to do.

Just then, as though she read my mind, my cell phone rings on the counter. It's a call from my best friend back home, Jess.

Smiling through the tears, I hit the answer button and hold the phone to my ear. "How'd you know I needed to hear a familiar voice right about now?"

Jess chuckles softly. I can almost picture her now. If I was still in Texas I'd be sitting across from her in her living room under a throw blanket while she looks back at me, effortlessly put together with her blonde hair in a messy bun on top of her head and a matching lounge set. Each of us would have a cup of coffee in hand.

"I told you we are soul sisters. I can't explain it, but something in my gut just told me I needed to call and check on you. How are things? Getting settled?"

I take a long breath and peer around at my cardboard box-covered kitchen. "Slowly. I was just getting ready to cry over a coffee mug."

"Sounds like I was right on time then. How are the kids?"

"Well, Maisie just signed up to do a Christmas play at church."

Jess gasps. "Oh my gosh, yes. I never thought of it, but she would be a perfect theater kid."

"She's dramatic enough, that's for sure."

"And Sadie?"

I pause, sticking my head out the swinging kitchen door to ensure no one is listening in on me. "She seems okay. I think she's a little nervous about starting school tomorrow." I admit. "Oh, Jess, I hate this for her. She had a good life back home. She finally had good friends, and she was in the band and had great grades. What a shitty thing to have to transfer during junior year."

"True, but Sadie's a tough kid. And she wanted to be with you, not Mark."

I nod, almost forgetting Jess can't see me. "I know. It's just that I wish she didn't have to experience any of this. I wish none of us did. Nolan seems the least bothered by it all, but I know he's probably struggling, too."

"You're all going to be okay." Jess reminds me gently. "I think getting settled into a small town and starting over won't be so bad. Besides, then you won't have to see Mark gallivanting around town with his girlfriend."

"Thank God for that."

"I saw them yesterday." She confesses. "They were jogging through the neighborhood. I was half tempted to hit him with my car, but knowing your luck, he's already removed you from his life insurance plan and she would get it all."

"Sadly, you're probably right." I tell her. "I'm proud of you for having self-control, though."

"I don't look great in orange. And I probably would not do well without a latte and a little sweet treat every afternoon," Jess confesses.

"Well, it's the thought that counts. So, I guess Brittani's new boob job must be healed then."

"You heard about that, huh?"

I groan. "Yes. I know I get alimony and child support, so I shouldn't complain, but I am still annoyed knowing that he just dropped all that money to buy his twenty-something year old girlfriend new boobs. Do you know who needs new boobs? Me, I'm the one that nursed three kids and am stuck walking around with two deflated balloons attached to my chest, but he sure never offered to buy me new ones."

"Don't worry. Eventually hers will be sad and droopy, too."

"Hopefully, you're right," I mumble.

Jess snickers as her husband's voice drifts in from the background. "Hey, I'm going to let you get back to unpacking, and we'll chat more later. Maybe the kids and I can come visit after the holidays."

I glance back at my mountain of boxes. "We'd love that. And

maybe I'll be done unpacking before then."

Chapter 4

"Okay, guys," I say to my two oldest children, as I put my SUV in park in front of *Fawn Creek Jr.-Sr. High School.* "Have a good day. Make good choices. Make some new friends and be nice to the weird kids. I love you."

"Be nice to Sadie, got it," Nolan confirms with a nod as he opens his door and steps out onto the pavement.

I turn to look at Sadie, who is glaring at her brother through the passenger side window. Her head turns slowly for her eyes to meet mine. "Why does he have to go to my school?"

I let out a sigh and send Sadie a sympathetic frown. "Unfortunately, Fawn Creek is too small of a town to have separate high school and junior high buildings." I remind her. "It'll be fine, Sadie. I'm sure you won't even see him. Remember, the principal said that they try to keep the two age groups separated as much as they can."

Sadie rolls her eyes. "We'll see about that," She mutters, opening her own door and stepping out onto the pavement.

Without another word, she closes her door and disappears into the school building. All three of my children are officially off to school for their first day, and I have the entire day to look for a job. But first, coffee.

I complete my drive through Fawn Creek and park in an empty

spot in front of Drip, Fawn Creek's adorable downtown coffee shop. I spotted this place the last time I came down to visit my parents, but thanks to Mark, I never got to stop. He turned his nose up at stopping at any coffee shop that wasn't a chain. I'm not sure why he thought chain coffee was better than a locally owned store, but it made no sense to me.

I swing open the glass door and step inside, taking it all in. Every part of this store was obviously meticulously decorated, with loving care, from the exposed brick walls to the dark stained wood floors and barn wood checkout counter.

"Hey! Welcome in!" A chipper voice from somewhere behind the counter calls out to me. I look around and try to determine the source of the sound when a slender woman wearing jeans, a Drip T-shirt and a black apron pops up from behind the counter. Her springy curls are wound up in a claw clip on the back of her head, and she smiles brightly.

"Morning," I greet her back, closing the distance between the two of us.

"What can I get started for you?"

I look at the menu. "Well, I've never been in before. Is there anything you recommend?"

The barista immediately perks up. "Well, my favorite right now is the Gingerbread latte. It has cinnamon, ginger, nutmeg and molasses. It's like Christmas in a cup."

I nod. "Okay. That sounds great. I'll take a medium." I decide, sliding my debit card across the counter towards her.

She rings me up and looks down at my card to read my name before handing it back to me. "Thank you, Reagan," she says, sliding the card back to me. "I'm Cassidy by the way, the owner of this little place. I'll have it ready in a jiff."

"Nice to meet you." I say, sliding the card back in my wallet.

"I love your shop. It's so cozy."

She beams. "Thanks! It was a lifelong dream of mine to leave the corporate world and open this place. I couldn't be happier with it."

As Cassidy gets to work on firing up the espresso machine, I walk around examining the rest of the store.

"So, you said this is your first time in. What brings you to Fawn Creek?" she asks, as she finishes crafting my drink.

"I actually grew up here and moved away years ago. My family and I just moved back last week."

Cassidy raises a brow and slides the cup across the counter to me. "Did you buy the cute little two-story house on Spring Street? The one with the wraparound porch?"

I nod. "That's me," I say, taking a sip of my drink. "Okay, this is incredible. I can see why it's your favorite."

"Glad you like it! And nice to meet you, neighbor. I live just a few houses down from you in the brick ranch-style house."

"Is that the one with the cactus-shaped mailbox?"

"That's us! Maybe once it warms up again, we can organize a neighborhood block party. My husband has no friends of his own, except for his golfing buddies, so I have to make all our friends for him."

I frown. "Well, I'd love to help, but I don't have a husband to offer. I left mine back in Houston."

Cassidy frowns. "Oh, I'm sorry."

"No, it's fine. It's for the best." I say, waving her off. "It's been kind of nice to start over and return to my roots. Plus, life is so much more affordable here than it was back there. I at least feel like I stand a chance at surviving as a single mom. Now, if I can just find a job. Any ideas?"

Cassidy pauses to think, drumming her fingers on the counter.

"Honestly, most places in town are family owned so they rarely have many openings or, even if they need help, they don't tend to pay super well. You could probably pick up some hours at the boutique or maybe at the grocery store. Otherwise, if you need something to support your family, you will probably have to travel out of town."

I sigh. "I was afraid you'd say that. Someone suggested that I could substitute teach. Any insight there?"

Cassidy perks up. "Oh, that's a good idea. The school pays well for substitutes, and you can kind of work around your kids' schedules."

I ponder the idea for a moment. "Don't you need a special license or something for that? I don't have any specialized training. I've been a stay at home mom for years now."

She waves me off. "Yes, but it's easy to get. I'm sure you could get started now and be ready to work after Christmas."

"Okay, who do I get a hold of for this? I really don't want to wait until after Christmas, but a plan is better than nothing."

"Just call the school and talk to Christy. She will get you all set up," Cassidy says, as the bell above the door chimes, alerting us to the fact that we have company.

Two Fawn Creek police officers walk in and wave hello to Cassidy.

"Hey, Derek. Hey Kyle." She greets them with the same bright smile she offered me. "What can I get you, fellas?"

I take another sip of my drink and begin to make my way out the door before calling back to her. "Thanks so much for your help! Have a great day!"

I grip my coffee as I step onto the sidewalk in the brisk fall air. Just in time to see Cash exit a pickup truck parked near the street.

"We meet again." I say with a smirk.

"Yeah, that's bound to happen in a town this size," he says with a cockeyed grin. "Getting settled?"

I nod. "Yeah, I got a lot of my unpacking finished yesterday. Now I just have to work through my massive to-do list."

"Anything I can help with?"

I frown. "Now that you mention it. Do you know any plumbers? I discovered this morning that I have a leak under my kitchen sink. I have a plastic bowl under it to catch the leak for now, but I need a plumber soon."

"I'll come take a look."

"Don't you have something more important to do? Like work?"

Cash shrugs. "I work at the oil refinery on a swing shift. I work four days on, three days off. Today just happens to be the beginning of my three days off. I went to the gym and now I'm coming to get a coffee, and then I'm headed home to tinker around in the garage with my bike. I've got the time."

I nod, grateful for his help, although I'm apprehensive to show it. "Okay, if you really don't mind. I don't want to be a burden."

"You're definitely not a burden," he assures me. "I'll get my coffee, grab some tools and meet you at your house soon."

Shit. Can I really handle being alone with Cash Hartwell?

* * *

"Okay, thank you, Christy. I'll be watching for your email." I say into my cell phone as I enter back into my kitchen. Pausing, I look down at Cash.

In the last hour he's already shown up to my house with tools in hand, ready to play Mr. Fix It and now he is elbow deep in the mess under my sink.

"Christy Crawford?" He asks, not removing his head from the kitchen cabinet.

I nod, although he can't see me. "Yes, at the school. She's going to email me paperwork to apply to be a substitute teacher," I say as I hop up to sit on the kitchen island near where he's working.

Cash climbs out from under the cabinet and sits up to face me. "I never pegged you to be the teacher type."

"Yeah, me neither." I admit with a shrug. "But, I have bills to pay, and this seems to be the best option for me to work around my kids' schedules."

He snickers and looks across the kitchen. "What are your kids going to think about you working at their school?"

I shrug. "Honestly, I don't care what they think. If they want food on the table and Wi-Fi, they are probably going to have to deal with it." I pause for a second to think. "Actually, Maisie would probably be excited to have me at her school. The other two, not so much, but like I said, they love their Wi-Fi."

Cash stands from the floor and faces me, wiping his hands on a nearby dishtowel. "Well, you are all fixed up. Just a loose pipe."

"Thanks. You're a lifesaver. What do I owe you?" I ask, sliding off the counter and moving towards my purse.

He shakes his head. "Nothing. It was no big deal."

I frown and turn back towards him. "Cash, you didn't have to do this, you know. I don't want you to feel like I'm taking advantage of your kindness."

He smirks. "I wanted to help. I enjoy knowing that you're taken care of."

My body tenses, unsure of what to say in response to his admission and suddenly very aware of the fact that he and I are alone together for the first time in years.

"Life sure knows how to throw you for a loop, doesn't it?" he says with a soft smile. "I always thought I'd be the one fixing things around your house... but I just assumed it'd be my house, too."

I freeze, tightening my grip on the countertop. "Cash..." I say, just above a whisper.

He shakes his head. "I know. I'm sorry. That was uncalled for. It's just... don't you ever wonder what life would be like if you hadn't disappeared?"

I frown back at him. "That's not fair, Cash. I didn't just disappear."

"Then what do you call it? You came home during spring break. You showed up at my house and asked me to take you for a ride in the sand hills like the good old days."

I shake my head, ready to defend myself to him, but he continues.

"Reagan, you kissed me. You told me you wanted me. We made love in the back of my truck, and then I dropped you off at your mom's house and never heard from you again."

I turn to face him. "Cash, we were broken up. I was young and stupid and vulnerable, and you were familiar, but I thought we had an understanding that we were done."

Cash pushes off the counter, closing the distance between us. "I was never done, Reagan. Not even when you married that white-collar pretty boy and moved to Houston." He shakes his head. "All I could do was hope that you'd come to your senses and come back to me."

I roll my eyes and cross my arms in front of my chest. "Oh

yeah, I'm sure you just waited around for all these years pining after me. I know you better than that, Cash. You were probably wrapped up with some other girl before I even left town."

Cash leans in even further. This time his face is so close to mine that our lips almost touch. "Yes, over the years I tried to move on. I tried to find someone who made me feel like you did. But no matter what, it wasn't enough. I love you, Reagan. I always have. I always will."

That's all it takes. His words hit me and I lean forward crashing into him. His familiar lips are kissing me just like they did when we were young. It's familiar. It's safe. And it's everything I've been craving for so long without even realizing it.

Cash places his hands on my hips and lifts me up to sit me back on the counter, still somehow not pulling his mouth away from mine.

I put my hands in his hair, gripping the strands between my fingers while steadying his face close to mine. His calloused hands glide under my shirt, gripping his fingertips into my bare skin. It takes everything within me not to let my own hands travel over his body. But, then, the ringing of my cell phone interrupts us.

Cash lets out a pained groan as he takes a step back.

"This can't be good," I mutter, heart sinking as I see the caller ID.

Fawn Creek High School.

I clear my throat and hit the speakerphone button. "Hello?"

"Um, yes. Mrs. Truitt?" The voice on the other end begins.

"Miller. It's Ms. Miller. I took back my maiden name after my divorce."

"Mrs. Miller." The woman on the other end corrects herself.

"Is this the parent or guardian of Nolan Truitt?"

"It is."

"This is Mrs. Bruce, the junior high principal. I have Nolan in my office. Do you have time to come in and visit? We have a bit of a... situation."

Chapter 5

"I cannot believe this." I say to my middle child, tossing my keys on the entryway table with a huff.

"Mom, I'm sorry! It was just a harmless prank!" Nolan says, following behind me.

"A harmless prank? You and your friends filled all the toilets in the boys' bathroom with foaming soap, baking soda and hydrogen peroxide! You caused the entire bathroom to flood and the suds to spill out into the hallway! And Mrs. Johnson nearly broke her hip by slipping in the suds. You're lucky a three-day suspension is all you got. And on your first day? Unbelievable."

"Mom, I said I'm sorry!"

"Where did you even get an idea like this?" I ask, running my hands through my hair.

He shrugs. "Science class. We did a volcano experiment today. The guys and I thought that a toilet volcano would be cool... and it really was."

I frown. "Well, what about being grounded? Is that cool?"

Nolan's jaw drops in shock. "Mom! That's not fair."

"Well, it's also not fair for you to get suspended on your first day of school in our new town, especially in the school district that I am trying to work for."

Nolan pauses. "Wait. What do you mean you're going to work

at my school?"

I let out a heavy sigh. "Well, I am possibly going to be substitute teaching at your school. I just need to fill out the paperwork and get a background check done. Of course, who knows if they will even want me there after the crap you pulled today."

"MOM. You can't work at my school." Nolan argues, wide-eyed as he shakes his head.

"What else would you like me to do? I need to bring in an income somewhere, and unless I want a half-hour commute to work out of town, which will result in you having to babysit every day, this is going to have to be sufficient."

Nolan pouts. "Fine. I'm going to my room." He says, turning towards the wooden staircase. Leave it to a teenager to make *me* feel like the bad guy after flooding his school.

"Don't touch the PlayStation!" I call out to him.

Nolan turns to face me, his jaw nearly reaching the floor. "Mom! That's not fair."

"Do you not understand what grounded means?" I ask, hands on my hips.

"What am I supposed to do for three days?"

I shrug. "Well, first, you can write an apology letter to the janitor for the mess you made. Then, I don't know, maybe I can find you some housework. Since you like playing in toilets so much, maybe you need to learn how to clean all of ours."

"Ew," he mutters with a wrinkle of his nose.

"Yeah, ew. Now, go get the game controllers and bring them back down." I demand.

Between Cash and Nolan, this is not how I expected our Monday to turn out.

* * *

I step out of the church on Wednesday night after dropping Maisie for her first night of play practice and into the parking lot as the cool breeze pierces through my wool sweater. I almost make it to my car when I spot a familiar motorcycle parked in the space next to me.

I grit my teeth as I close the distance between us. We haven't spoken since Monday, when we had our throwback groping session on my kitchen counter. Now, I'm not sure how I'm supposed to talk to him. I am way too old for a man to cause me this much anxiety.

"Hey," Cash says, his gruff voice sending a shiver down my spine that I cannot attribute to the weather.

"Hi." I reply, wrapping my arms in front of my chest to protect myself from the wind.

"So. Are we going to talk about what happened in your kitchen on Monday?" He asks, moving closer to me, ignoring the fact that anyone in town could see us here.

"Yes. I'm sorry, I've been a little busy."

Cash removes his leather jacket and drapes it over my shoulders. Then he rubs his hands along my arms as though attempting to warm me from the friction. "Yeah, I heard all about what your kid did at school," he says with a chuckle. "What an epic prank."

I let out a groan. "Yeah, epic is not exactly the word I would use. Someone could have gotten hurt. And it made such a big mess. I'm still pretty mad at him."

Cash smirks. "Kids do dumb shit sometimes, Rae. Do I need to remind you of the time that you and I dumped a Costco-sized box of instant mashed potatoes all over the high school lawn right before it rained for three days straight?"

I grimace. "I forgot all about that."

Cash goes on. "Yeah, the principal sure didn't. In fact, every time I see that man, he still brings up the fact that it took the maintenance team two leaf blowers, three shop vacs and a snow shovel to get it all off the grass before it killed the sod. Not to mention the fact that it smelled like butter for weeks."

I shake my head, nearly experiencing the smell of the butter-flaked potatoes all over again. "We were such morons. We thought the sprinklers would just wash it all away. Instead, it turned into a swampy mess that nearly ruined the lawn in time for prom walk-in. They really shouldn't have let us graduate."

Cash chuckles. "See? The apple doesn't fall too far from the tree, does it? You have to admit, it's kind of funny."

I sigh. "It would be a hell of a lot funnier if I weren't the one dealing with the aftermath all alone. Parenting is not for the weak."

"Rae, you aren't alone." Cash whispers, barely audible. "At least you don't have to be."

I snicker. "Oh really, what are you suggesting? You want to take on all of this?" I ask, waving in the general direction of my body.

"Hell yes, I do." He replies with a sly smile, as he pulls me close. He sounds as though he's considering undressing me in the church parking lot.

I roll my eyes. "Cash, I don't think you know what you're getting into. I'm not that cute little 17-year-old girl that you used to make out with in a cornfield in your truck. I have kids and a very messy divorce under my belt. Not to mention the twenty pounds I've gained since then and the stretch marks and the gray hair and let's not get started on the perimenopause that I'm way too young to be experiencing already...."

Before I can continue, Cash steps towards me and places his hand around the back of my neck, pulling my mouth to his. He kisses me deeply and passionately until he finally pulls away.

"I have to get inside. I promised Mom I would help build sets for the play. Hopefully that answered your question. But if it didn't, let me make myself perfectly clear. Yes, Reagan, I am sure that I want you. And if we are being honest, your thirty-eight-year-old body is even hotter than your nineteen-year-old one was. In fact, your body is all I've been thinking about for days now."

I find myself blushing as he finishes his speech, grateful for the dimly lit parking lot enabling me to hide my bright pink cheeks from him.

He leans forward to kiss me again. "Any questions?"

I smirk before gently pushing him away. "No. Now go. The last thing we need is for your mom to be mad at us because you're late. I don't want to get on her bad side."

"You could never be on her bad side. I'll come by and see you later this week, and maybe we can finish... something." He says with a wink before turning away from me and walking towards the church.

"Looking forward to it." I call back.

* * *

The alarm on my phone screams through my dimly lit bedroom, telling me it's time once again to drag my children from their beds for school. Christmas break can't come fast enough.

Honestly, if we could just get past our first Christmas without Mark, life will surely get easier, right?

I didn't sleep worth a crap last night, of course; I laid in bed and stared at the ceiling until two in the morning, replaying my conversation with Cash over and over in my head. And don't even get me started on our spur-of-the-moment make out session on my kitchen counter Monday morning.

What do I even do from here? When I married Mark and moved to Texas, I just assumed that Cash was where he belonged, in my past. I never imagined I'd be back here, and finding myself falling for him all over again... that is... if I ever actually fell out of love with him to begin with. Two years ago I'd say I had, but now? I'm not so sure.

I swing my legs over the side of the bed and carry my phone into the hall to begin the process of waking up the kids. I knock on Sadie's door, and she answers immediately.

"I'm up! I've been up for an hour." She groans.

I nod at the closed door. "Okay." I say before moving on to Nolan's room. It's his first day back since his little science experiment.

Just as I raise my fist to knock, the phone rings. It's the high school. What could they want now? Maybe they decided they don't want Nolan back after all. What if he's expelled and I have to home school him? Neither of us would survive that.

"Hello." I say, pressing the phone against my ear, bracing myself for the worst.

"Hi, Reagan. It's Christy at the school. I was calling to see if you would be available to substitute for the high school math teacher today."

I pause, racking my brain. Aside from hoping for a nap after my sleepless night last night, I have nothing else going on today.

And let's be honest, I could use the money.

"Yes, I'd love to. I didn't expect all of my paperwork to be back so quickly." I confess.

"Your background check came back clear late last night. Just in time. We're in enough of a crunch that we are able to hire subs without worrying about licensing requirements. I don't want to scare you off, but between us and the grade school, we should be able to keep you nice and busy."

"That's great news, Christy. Okay, I'd better go get ready. I'll see you a bit before eight."

"Perfect! See you then."

I hit the disconnect button on my phone and knock on Nolan's door. "Hey, kid. Back to school today. And even better news, Mommy will be there to make sure you stay out of trouble."

"Isn't taking away my PlayStation punishment enough?" Nolan grumbles from behind the closed door. Sounds like today is going to be just peachy.

* * *

My first two hours of the day fly by with only a few occasional hiccups. As it turns out, substituting is not as hard as I thought it would be. Mostly, the teacher I'm subbing for, Mrs. Hiner, left me everything I needed to be successful, and basically I'm doing more babysitting than mathematics. Thank goodness, because if there's one thing I know for sure, I know that I'm not qualified to be a math teacher. Especially considering the fact that I had to take Algebra three times.

Of course, based on the class roster for my third-hour students, there is a good chance that my easy day could go south real quick.

Just as I'm working to psych myself up, Sadie steps into the doorway of the classroom and freezes in her tracks to stare me down. She does not look happy to see me.

"Good morning, Miss Truitt." I address her with a smirk.

Sadie snarls. "Seriously, you're MY teacher? Isn't this illegal or something?"

"I don't think so." I answer with a shrug as I sit on the corner of the desk behind me.

Sadie rolls her eyes. "Well, it should be."

"Feel free to write a letter to your senator during your lunch break then." I retort. "I told you I was going to be here today."

"Yes, but you didn't tell me you were subbing in my precalculus class. Do you even know how to do precalculus?" She challenges, raising a brow. "I remember when you helped me with Math in the fourth grade. That's when I got my first F."

I glance down at the stack of papers sitting on top of the open manila folder labeled *Sub Plans*. Just the worksheet itself gives me anxiety, but the thought of actually teaching it is impossible.

"Well, no. But, I was given clear instructions to pass out these papers, and let you work on them independently. If anyone has questions, save them for tomorrow when your teacher returns."

Sadie rolls her eyes. "Fine," she mutters, just as a group of boys walk into the room. They take their seats behind Sadie, barely getting into the room before the bell rings.

"Whoa." A boy with permed hair and braces says just above a whisper to his friends. "The sub today is hot."

Sadie rolls her eyes dramatically and turns to face them. "The sub today is my mom." She informs them. "And everyone says I look just like her, so what are you saying, Lyle?"

"I... uh..." the boy stumbles over his words, trying to come up with a response, but ultimately failing. I speak up and save him.

"Okay, now that we've determined how strong my genetics really are, let's get started..." I announce to the room. "My name is Ms. Miller, and I'll be your sub today. Let's get to work, shall we?"

Chapter 6

The soft hum of Christmas carols rings through the house, hopefully setting the tone for this evening. Since I wasn't needed at work today, much to Sadie's delight, I spent the day shopping for new seasonal decor in Owen, the nearest large town.

Once home, I found a crackling fireplace scene to play on the TV while I worked away on setting up my new artificial tree.

I wish I could be the type of person who had a real tree for Christmas, and once upon a time I gave it a shot. But, it wasn't long before I grew tired of sweeping up needles and of course I forgot to water it, resulting in a dead spruce long before our holiday festivities started. Ever since then, I've been an artificial tree kind of mom.

I had a beautiful tree in my last house, but that house had vaulted ceilings and could handle a twelve-foot tree. This space, on the other hand, has standard eight-foot ceilings, and the massive tree, like many other things, had to be left behind.

Now, my halls are decked, the best they could be on a budget, and all that's left is for the kids to decorate the tree tonight. At least I thought to rescue my box of keepsake ornaments from the attic that I've collected from the kids over the years. Memories of the three of them hanging the ornaments that they brought home each year for Mark and me, flood my brain. What a simple time. It almost feels as though it was a lifetime ago.

The chime of the doorbell causes me to snap out of my daydreams. I make my way towards the door and swing it open to find Cash standing on the porch. The sound of the lightly falling snow behind him causes me to pause and take in the entire scene.

However, he doesn't let me pause for long. Instead, he steps forward, using one hand to hold a sprig of mistletoe over my head and the other hand to wrap around my waist and pull me in close to him. He kisses me deeply and passionately, like a hunger that he's been aching to satisfy for years. And maybe he has.

After a short time, I'm the first to take a step back. "Well, hello to you, too," I say with a smirk.

"I've been thinking of doing that since Wednesday," he admits, leaning forward to kiss me again. This time, softer and with more patience as though we do this every day.

"The mistletoe was a nice touch. Completely unnecessary, but festive." I say with a chuckle. "Want to come in so the neighbors aren't getting a free show?" I offer, nodding towards the house across the street. Cash follows my gaze to see an overly curious white-haired woman who is dressed in a bathrobe and blatantly spying on us through an opening in her curtain.

"I'd love to," Cash replies obviously with more than talking on his mind. He leans to the side and picks up a cup carrier from the small table next to my door. "I stopped for hot cocoa, too. Just the way you like it, with a touch of peppermint."

I close the door behind him and follow him to the sofa, where he hands me my cup. "Cash, I can't believe you remembered how I take my hot cocoa." I whisper.

"I remember everything." He smirks. "We have a lot of

history, you and I."

"That we do." I agree, taking a sip and letting the minty chocolate slide down my throat. "I thought Drip closes at 1:00. How'd you manage to get away with hot drinks at nearly two in the afternoon?"

He shrugs. "What can I say? Aunt Cassidy loves me. She was still there closing up for the day and was more than willing to help me try to impress a pretty girl."

"Wait. Cassidy's your aunt? How did I not know that?"

"I bet you'd remember her if you thought about it. But she worked a lot back in our day. She had a demanding office job and a young daughter, Sierra, when you left town so she wasn't around much. Besides, we were both a couple of self-absorbed teenagers back then, to be honest."

I nod. "Yeah we were, weren't we?"

Cash places his cup on the coffee table before turning to face me. Slowly, he reaches over to pick up and squeeze my hand. A soft smile spreads across his face, causing him to look almost exactly like the boy I was so head over heels with all those years ago. The boy I swore I'd marry one day. The one I was sure to spend the rest of my life with.

"What are you thinking, Rae?"

I shake my head, placing my cup next to his. "Nothing really. Just us, and all the time we've spent together."

"I love when history repeats itself," he says with a smirk.

His words cause me to blush, which I admit I seem to be doing a lot these days when it comes to him.

"Cash, are you sure this is what you want? I mean, you've had a couple of days to think it over. No one would blame you if you wanted to keep living and enjoying your carefree, bachelor pad life instead of taking on a mom with three kids. One of which who is probably going to end up leading a prison gang at some point in his life."

Cash squeezes my hand. "Reagan. Yes, I have thought about this over and over since Wednesday. Hell, I've been thinking about it since I heard you were moving back to town. Yes, I want to be with you. You and your crazy crew of kids. If you're all in, so am I. Besides maybe I can help keep your crazy middle child out of jail and teach him a few things."

I lean in and kiss his awaiting lips gently before pulling back to look at him. "Are we really doing this? After all these years?"

"We're really doing this," he confirms.

"I wonder how long it'll take for word to get around town."

Cash snickers. "It probably already has, thanks to the security woman across the street. I'm surprised my mom hasn't called me yet."

Just then, as if on cue, Cash's phone vibrates in his coat pocket. The word *MOM* flashes across his screen.

I gasp and slap my hand over my mouth, fighting back a laugh. "Surely, word didn't travel that fast."

Cash laughs. "Girl, it's been way too long since you left home."

* * *

"You got a tree!" Maisie exclaims as soon as she walks into the house, dropping her backpack in the entryway. "I thought maybe you wouldn't get one this year."

"You thought I wouldn't get a tree?" I repeat with a frown. "Why wouldn't I?"

She shrugs off her coat and hangs it near the door. "I don't know. Dad isn't here. I thought maybe we wouldn't have

Christmas since we're poor now."

With that, Maisie turns and walks towards the kitchen to undoubtedly locate a snack, not even noticing that she's left me in the entryway completely flabbergasted.

"Maisie, we aren't poor." Sadie calls to her, rolling her eyes.

"Well, what do you call it then?" Nolan pipes up. "I mean, Mom is working at the school now as a substitute. Mom's never had a job before."

"Because Mom has never had to work!" Sadie argues, now starting to sound a bit heated. "That doesn't mean we're poor. That means she is taking care of our family. There's a difference."

"Okay!" I shout, walking into the center of the room to get the attention of all my children. "That's enough arguing about me while I'm standing right here. Here are the facts. No, we are not poor. We don't have money to throw around like we once did, but otherwise we are fine. You guys don't worry about our finances. That's my job. Yes, I do have to work now, but it's okay. I enjoy it. I actually wonder if I should have become a teacher a long time ago. Yes, we are still having Christmas. And tonight, we are going to decorate the tree, drink hot cocoa, have a good dinner and watch a movie together like we do every year. Okay?"

Nolan wrinkles his nose. "Do I have to help decorate the tree? Isn't that a girl's job?"

I furrow my brow. "Nolan James. There is no such thing as a girl's job or a boy's job. They are all just jobs. Besides, this isn't work. It's family togetherness time."

"Family time IS work." Nolan mutters under his breath as he stomps toward the sofa, nearly knocking into Maisie as she walks back into the room, biting into an apple. They both plop

46

down on the same couch cushion at once.

"Nolan, move over," Maisie squeals, pushing his arm. "Mom, tell him I was here first."

I let out a huff. "Nolan, please. Give your sister some space."

"Fine," he grumbles, scooting over to the other end of the couch. "What time does all this family fun start, anyway?"

"Why, do you have a date or something?" Maisie teases.

"A date with his PlayStation." Sadie answers.

"I'm still grounded from my PS4." He tells his sisters before shooting me a sideways glance.

"Whose fault is that?" Sadie asks with a laugh. "Maybe you shouldn't have been playing Mad Scientist with the school toilets."

"That was five days ago! When are you people going to drop it already? Everyone at school was talking about it today, too."

"The kids at school will move on as soon as they have something new to talk about." I tell him with a shrug. "Your family, however, will never forget."

* * *

"Mom, can I call Dad before we decorate the tree?" Maisie asks me across the dinner table as she devours the last bite of her cinnamon roll.

The sound of Maisie's request makes my stomach turn. My night of family fun has already been soiled by the kids arguing and worrying about our finances. Now we want to throw Mark into the mix?

"Yes, of course." I tell her as I use the center of my cinnamon roll to soak up the last bit of my chili. Over the last few years, it has become our tradition to decorate the tree after having chili and cinnamon rolls for dinner. We then use the remaining rolls for breakfast the following morning. It's quickly become a favorite family meal.

Maisie carries her dishes to the sink and before returning to me to intercept my phone. I hand the device over, and she scrolls to his name, placing the call like a pro.

"Hi, Daddy!" she exclaims happily when he answers the call. "Guess what? I'm going to be in my first play. Can you come watch it? It's right before Christmas." Maisie pauses to listen to his response before handing the phone over to me. "He wants to talk to you," she says with a scowl, obviously deflated from her father's lack of excitement.

Fantastic. As if this night could get any worse. Mark and I can rarely converse anymore without arguing.

I swallow hard and brace myself for the worst as I grip the phone and bring it to my ear. "Hello?"

"Reagan, hey," Mark responds gruffly. "What's this about a play?"

I look at Maisie, offering her a soft smile, before replying to him. "Um, yeah. Maisie is in a play at the church. They will perform on the Sunday before Christmas."

"I see."

I hold a finger up to Maisie before excusing myself to leave the room. Once I step onto the porch, wrapping myself in my coat, I continue my conversation. "What's your plan for the holidays? Our divorce paperwork says you get them from Christmas afternoon until New Year's Day."

Mark groans. "Yeah, I'm not going to be able to keep them for a week. Brittani and I have things going on. I can see if I can reschedule, but..."

"No, it's fine." I answer quickly.

And *it is* fine. I'd rather not worry about my kids being in Houston for a week with no supervision for the week while he is at work. It's too bad since I'm sure they were looking forward to going back home and seeing their friends. But, I've never been away from the kids longer than a long weekend trip with Mark, and I'm not ready to start yet.

"I think we can make the play, though. We will bring their gifts and do our the exchange with the kids after church if that's okay."

"We?" I ask, although I already know the answer.

"Brittani and I, of course. She would be with me. She's excited to see the kids and she even helped pick out their presents."

I roll my eyes. Of course, she did. Why wouldn't their father have shopped for them instead?

"Sounds like a plan, Mark. I'll let the kids know about the change in plans."

"Thanks, Reagan. Also, I think I found Sadie a car there in Fawn Creek that I could get her for her birthday. It would be easier than buying something and bringing it there myself. Do you have someone that you trust to look at it first? Maybe a local mechanic?"

I pause, my mind immediately going to Cash, making a mental note to text him tonight and see if he can help. "I'm sure I can find someone."

"Great. I'll send you the listing, and if it's good to go, I'll get with them about the payment. I promised I'd get her a car for her birthday, so I don't want to let her down."

"Sounds good." I mutter. "I'll let you know how it goes."

I roll my eyes and disconnect the call. As if he hasn't done enough to let them down.

* * *

"Can I be done now?" Nolan whines as I step back to admire our newly decorated tree.

The kids have spent the last thirty minutes layering our new tree with my entire collection of keepsake ornaments. Over the past seventeen years, I've had so many decorations pile up, from pictures of the kids laminated on handmade snowflakes to clear ornaments with their painted fingerprints turned into snowmen and reindeer and Santa. They easily filled the entire tree with no need for anything else.

"Yes, Nolan. Please go on up to your room and save yourself from this awful family time."

"Gladly," he says with a groan, barely pausing before running up the stairs.

Sadie and I exchange a look as I take a seat on the sofa. "You're free to go, too. I remember being a teenager. I guess I didn't love family time all that much either."

"And miss the end of *The Grinch*? Are you out of your mind?" Sadie replies with a smirk. "It's fine. I want to stay and watch the movie. Sorry, Nolan's such a twerp."

I offer her a soft smile. "It's okay. I'm sure the fact that you guys aren't going to Houston isn't helping matters much either. Sorry, kid. I know you were looking forward to it."

Sadie waves me off. "It's fine. Honestly, I think I'd rather be here anyway. I've made some new friends at school, and I'll have time to hang out with them a bit. Besides, Dad's coming to visit, and at least we will get to celebrate with him. And I won't have to spend a week with him and Brittani. I'm still mad at him anyway."

I frown at my daughter before reaching over to squeeze her hand. "Thank you."

"For what?"

I shrug. "For being you. I know this past year hasn't been easy, but you have handled everything with so much grace. Honestly, I don't feel like I've given you enough credit for being as levelheaded as you have been. I love you. Hopefully, we can make up for it this weekend when we celebrate your birthday."

"I love you, too, Mom. And whatever we do will be perfect. I promise."

I take a long sip of my drink and look around our living room. It's completely dark except for the tree and the glow of the television. This may not be the Christmas I expected this year, but this might be the exact one we needed.

Chapter 7

"Mom, are you sure you don't mind keeping Nolan and Maisie for the night?"

"Yes, of course," my mother assures me as she stands at her kitchen island, removing the last few chocolate chip cookies from the baking sheet. "We are going to have a great night."

I nod before reaching across the counter to steal a cookie for myself. "Thank you, really. I want Sadie to have a great time celebrating her birthday with her friends. If I can just focus on her, instead of trying to keep the other two entertained, that will be a big help."

"So, what do you have planned?"

"Well, it'll be Sadie and two girls she goes to school with, Becca and Courtney. We are going to go to Owen for the night. The plan is sushi, ice skating, a carriage ride. Then, we will finish off with hot cocoa while we drive through the park to see the Christmas lights."

"A good old-fashioned Christmas birthday celebration," My mom declares. "Is Sadie excited?"

I nod. "Yes. She has been the easiest kid throughout all of this. She's really stepped up to help around the house and with her siblings. I just want to make her birthday really special."

Mom looks to the backyard where Nolan and Maisie are

playing catch with her dog, Bingo. "Has she heard from Mark?"

I roll my eyes. "I don't know, honestly. He sent me a link to a car that he wants to buy her for her birthday. He wants me to have someone go check it out and make sure it's good to go."

My mom pauses. "Do you need your dad to go look?"

"No, I... um... I asked someone already. They are going to take a look today."

She raises an eyebrow. "Would this someone be Cash Hartwell?"

Immediately, I feel my face grow warm. *Busted.* "Maybe."

"So it's true? You two are dating?" The smirk on her face makes it very clear that this is not news to her. She's obviously already heard through the Fawn Creek pipeline.

"Yes," I confirm, "it's all very new. Like yesterday, new."

She chuckles. "It's not exactly new. You've been in love with that boy since you were old enough to drive. What do the kids think?"

I pause, glancing back outside to ensure my children are out of earshot. "They don't really know yet," I admit, to my mother's horror. "I will tell them eventually, maybe tomorrow night. Honestly, I was planning to tell them last night, and then Mark dropped the bomb about not taking them over Christmas break. So, I decided that was enough emotional whiplash for one day."

"Better tell them soon before someone else in town does. Word travels fast around here."

"Oh, believe me, I've noticed," I say, taking a bite of my cookie. "Some things never change."

* * *

"Sadie, are you about ready to go?" I call to her up the stairs.

"Don't forget your hat and gloves!"

"Be right there!" She calls down to me just as my phone vibrates in my pocket.

Cash: I looked over the car, and drove it several miles on the highway. It's a solid ride. If it were my kid, I'd be okay with her driving it.

Reagan: Good. That's exactly what I wanted to hear. Okay, let the guy know that I'll have my ex get in touch with him for the payment. I really appreciate you doing this for me. I wouldn't know the first thing about buying a used car.

Cash: I'm happy to help. Can't wait to see how she likes it.

Quickly, I fire off a text to Mark and slide the phone back into my pocket as Sadie makes her way down the stairs. She smiles softly at me as we make eye contact.

"You ready?"

"Yes! I texted the girls and told them we are on the way. I can't believe Owen has an ice skating rink right in the middle of downtown."

"Don't forget about the horse drawn carriage rides!"

"Right! And carriage rides. This is so cool. Like a real-life Hallmark movie."

"Well, what are we waiting for? Let's go check it out."

* * *

I look back from my seat in the middle of the horse-drawn carriage, watching as my daughter and her two new besties enjoy taking in the Christmas lights in downtown Owen. It's been a busy evening. We devoured more sushi than I would have ever expected a middle-aged woman and a few teenage girls to put away. Then, the girls attempted to ice skate, while I watched from a safe distance behind the barrier wall. It's been so much fun and Sadie has seemed to enjoy every second. I might even dare to call it a perfect night.

"Alright, ladies, I hope you had a great time," Deserai, the carriage driver, tells us as she brings the horses to a stop at her tent.

"We did!" The girls answer in a chorus as we all climb down from the carriage and find our footing on the pavement.

We thank Deserai and then make our way back towards the ice rink to clear room on the sidewalk for the next group of riders.

"Well, girls, anything else we want to do before we go for a drive through the Christmas lights?" I ask.

"Can we get hot cocoa first?" Sadie asks, pointing at a coffee truck parked nearby.

"Of course," I say, causing the girls to race towards the unsuspecting barista before I can even finish my sentence.

We place our orders and step back to wait for our drinks to be made, when I hear Sadie's phone chime in her pocket.

"I wonder why Dad's texting me." She mutters as she opens the message and reads it just below her breath. "A car?!" she squeals. "Mom, did you know Dad got me a car?"

I wince. *Couldn't he have waited until tomorrow?* "Yes, I knew."

"And you didn't tell me?" Sadie's mouth is hanging open in shock.

"Well, I wanted to make sure everything was going to work out first. I had someone go look at it today and I reported back to your dad that it was a good choice for you. Since then, I haven't heard a word."

"Well, it's parked at our house. The keys are in the mailbox. Can we please go home and see it? I can't wait to drive it."

The excitement in Sadie's voice cuts right through me. Of course, I'm happy for her. She deserves a car. She's a good student and never gives me any trouble. Besides her having a car means she can help me get her siblings where they need to go, too. However, I can't help but feel a little deflated. I worked hard organizing this evening, and leave it to Mark to overshadow me even from another state.

I hold up a hand. "Slow down. Let's get our drinks and drive through the lights, and then we will head home to check it out."

Sadie frowns. "Can we just skip the Christmas lights?"

I furrow my brows. "You want to skip the lights? Seriously? You always loved seeing the Christmas light display at John-stone Park when we came to visit Grandma and Grandpa for Christmas."

"Mom, please? The lights are the same as last year. And I have a car waiting at home for me."

Just as Sadie finishes her speech, the barista slides the last of our cups across the counter, interrupting the tension and says, "There you go. Enjoy!"

We thank him, grab our drinks and make our way towards the car, with Sadie nearly skipping ahead of me.

I call out to her. "Sadie, I have to check with your dad and see if you have insurance on the car before you go driving off into the sunset. So, no guarantees about it tonight."

Sadie turns to me, holding up her phone to show me a screenshot. "He already sent me a copy of the insurance card. Everything is good, Mom! Maybe I can even drive Becca and Courtney home. I'm so pumped. This is the best gift ever."

The drive back to Fawn Creek from Owen is painfully different from the drive towards Sadie's birthday celebration. All the way to Owen the girls had chatted about boys and their favorite kind of sushi and how they were looking forward to ice skating.

The drive back buzzes with a different excitement. Excitement of a new car and of freedom. The night I worked so hard to give Sadie is long forgotten, and once again I've been overshadowed by Mark.

I turn the corner to our house, and Sadie gasps from the passenger seat as the sight of her rust-orange Dodge Nitro comes into view. "There it is! It's so cute!"

I have to admit, she's right. It is really cute and something I could see myself driving as a teenage girl. Honestly, it's even cuter than the listing made it out to be.

I park my Tahoe and climb out, waiting in the driveway as the girls get the keys from the mailbox and rush to climb inside. They pause only long enough for me to get a photo of Sadie with the car before they are all belted in and ready to roll.

"Mom, we're going to Sonic to show this thing off!" Sadie announces with glee. "Love you!"

I nod, trying to hide my disappointment. "Okay. Love you, too. Home by midnight and be careful, please."

I hate to admit it, but even with seeing how excited she is, I'm disappointed. But what else can I do? It's insured, Sadie showed me the screenshot herself. Cash said it's safe to drive. And, Sadie is a great driver with a license. I guess all I can really do is let her go.

I watch Sadie's taillights disappear into the distance and pull out my phone. Before I even know what I'm doing, I'm standing in the street reaching out to a familiar voice.

"Hello?" Cash answers on the second ring.

"Hey. What are you doing?" I ask, kicking at a piece of loose gravel in the middle of the street.

He chuckles. "What I always do on the weekend... working on my bike. What're you doing? I thought you'd still be in the middle of a birthday extravaganza."

"Same," I admit. "Mark texted Sadie just as we were headed to look at Christmas lights to tell her that the car had been dropped off at the house. We couldn't get home fast enough."

"Did she like it?" he asks. The sound of metal on metal clings in the background as he continues to work.

"She loves it. I think she loves the idea of having a car even more. She was so ready to get in it and drive off into the sunset with her friends."

"You sound disappointed." He notes, and the clanging stops.

"I am. Listen, I know it's petty, but I'm annoyed. I had this night all planned out. We were supposed to come home and continue the night. I had snacks and movies and face masks for the girls for their sleepover. Instead, Mark sprung the car on her without telling me it was going to be delivered today. Now they are off at Sonic and I'm home alone."

"You want some company? I'm great at eating snacks, but I have to draw the line at face masks."

* * *

By the time Cash knocks on the front door, I'm already in my comfy clothes and huddled under a blanket on the sofa while a movie is starting. An array of snacks is spread out on the table in front of me.

"Come in!" I call out to him, hoping he will hear me so I won't have to leave my comfort zone. I'm successful.

"Hey," he greets me with a wide smile before kicking off his shoes and meeting me on the couch. "Empty house tonight, or are the two non-drivers up in their rooms?"

I shake my head. "They're at my mom's. And Sadie has a midnight curfew, so I'm sure she will be gone until 11:59 and 57 seconds." I motion for him to join me. "And as much as I'd love for you to meet them, let's be a little more intentional about it. Maybe at the parade on Thursday? That seems a little easier than Sadie coming in to find us on the couch together tonight. It's been a big enough night for her."

"Deal. I promise to be gone by midnight." He agrees as he takes a seat next to me. He places his arm around my shoulders and pulls me close. "How do you feel about her newfound freedom? Is it weird?"

"A little," I admit. "Truly, she's a good kid. I trust her. I just... didn't expect her to turn seventeen and suddenly grow up so fast."

"I can unhook her battery when she gets home if you want me to." He offers with a smirk.

I laugh and playfully smack his chest. "No, this is more of a me problem than a Sadie problem."

"Okay, but I mean it. You just say the word. If you ever need her to spend more time at home, I'll do it."

"I'll keep that in mind," I say, snuggling in closer to him.

"What are we watching?" Cash asks, turning towards the TV and wrapping an arm around me. "A Christmas Story?"

"My favorite." I say with a grin.

He shakes his head. "Oh, I remember when you used to make me watch this every weekend from Thanksgiving until Christmas."

"I can't help it. It's a comfort thing."

"Like that sweatshirt you're wearing?" He teases, as he tugs gently on the bottom hem. "My sweatshirt."

I furrow my brows and look down at my beloved and stained Fawn Creek Prairie Dogs sweatshirt. "Excuse me? You're obviously mistaken. This is mine."

Cash shakes his head. "Reagan, only if you stealing it nearly twenty years ago means that you own it. That was mine, and I let you borrow it one night. Then I never got it back. Remember? The night over Spring Break when it started snowing?"

I pause, thinking back to that night when Cash and I were hanging out at his house. I had on a T-shirt and a pair of shorts because it was nearly eighty degrees that day. But when we walked outside for him to drive me home, there was half a foot of snow on the ground. He handed me his sweatshirt, and I put it on over my clothes. The rest was apparently history.

"Oops." I laugh, remembering how I slept in this sweatshirt that night because it smelled like him. In hindsight, it makes sense why this has always been the first shirt I put on when I'm sad or overwhelmed. It's like my very own security sweatshirt... with a prairie dog on it. "Do you want it back?"

He shakes his head. "No, it looks much better on you. Besides, I like seeing you like this. In your comfy shirt and pajama pants. I feel like it means that you're still comfortable around me."

I shrug. "I am. There's something to be said for picking up where you left off years ago. We can avoid the whole awkward getting-to-know-you stage. You already know what I look like without makeup on. Hell, you even got to see the old and updated version of that when you startled me into spilling pickle juice all over the grocery store."

"It still reeks of brine in there, by the way." He adds with a laugh.

"You know me. I'm pretty good at leaving my mark wherever

I go."

"That you do, Reagan Miller. That you do."

Chapter 8

"Hey, I'm standing in front of the police station. Where are you?" I ask into my phone as my eyes scan up and down Main Street looking for any sign of Cash.

"I'm just about to walk out of Drip. I got you a hot cocoa, hopefully you don't mind."

"Cash, have you ever known me to be a girl that turns down chocolate?" I laugh in response as I walk down the sidewalk toward Drip. "I'll meet you outside."

I hang up the phone and slide it into my coat pocket as I continue my trek down the sidewalk. That is, until I meet up with my son.

"Hey, Mom." Nolan greets me as I approach him. He's sitting on the curb with two other teenage boys, waiting for the parade to start. He stands and moves towards me, meeting me on the sidewalk.

"Hey, I'm going to walk down to the coffee shop to meet Cash. Can I trust you to be left unsupervised?"

Nolan's face immediately turns beet red. "Mom! Yes, I'm not a baby." He looks back at his friends as though making sure they didn't overhear me.

"I never said you were. I'm more worried about you trying to pull off another epic prank while I'm not around."

My son rolls his eyes. "I haven't had my PS4 in over a week. I'm not going to do anything stupid to keep me from getting it back as soon as possible."

"I hope you mean it." I tell hi, with a smirk as I turn to finish my journey towards the coffee shop. Admittedly, I can't help but feel as though I've just experienced a parenting win. My kid actually learned a lesson. Maybe there is some hope for my crazy middle child after all. A girl can dream at least.

I reach Drip just as Cash steps out the door, holding two to-go cups in his gloved hands. As soon as he spies me, he grins so wide that the smile reaches his eyes. Just like he used to when we were sixteen.

"Hi," he whispers as we meet, and he hands me my cup. "Been waiting long?"

"Nope. Just got here." I assure him.

"Can I kiss you? Are we okay to do that in public now?" Cash asks in a hushed tone as he leans into me.

"I would be offended if you didn't, actually."

With that, Cash rests a gloved hand on the back of my neck and pulls me in for a kiss. What I assume would have been a tender moment quickly escalates as soon as his mouth finds mine. If it weren't for the sound of far-off police sirens, a ten-minute warning that the parade is about to start, I may have forgotten where we were altogether.

"Sounds like the parade is starting soon," I say with a grin, biting my bottom lip. "Can we go stand closer to the police station? That's where Nolan is with his friends, and I want to keep an eye on him."

"Of course." Cash shrugs, following my lead.

"Are you nervous about meeting the kids tonight?" I ask, turning to look back at him as we walk along.

"No, not at all. Should I be?" he asks, raising a brow.

I shake my head. "No. They all know about you, and they are all excited to meet you. However, don't be surprised if Nolan asks to drive your motorcycle. I already told him no. Twice."

"Maybe we can go for a short ride when the weather clears up. If that's okay?"

"That's fine. Just know that he will probably want a ride every day after you do it once. Hell, you might have to help him build his own dirt bike one day."

"What do you think of that?"

I shrug. "Honestly, if it gets him out of his room and off his PlayStation, it might not be a bad thing. As long as you make sure the bike can't go too fast."

I stop on the sidewalk and nudge Cash, pointing to where Nolan is still sitting on the curb. "Speak of the devil."

He has a plastic grocery bag in his hand, ready to fill with candy, and suddenly he doesn't seem like as much of a sweaty, ornery teenage boy. Instead, he looks like my sweet little guy that I used to dress in Christmas sweaters and take to the mall to take his photo with Santa. I miss those days, but also, I wish I could do a better job of enjoying this new stage of his life, too.

"Which one is he?" Cash whispers.

"The middle one. In the Under Armour hoodie."

"Where's his coat?" Cash snickers.

I roll my eyes. "In my Tahoe. I tried to make him wear it. I told him it would be cold, but he's a teenage boy. God forbid any of his friends find out that he owns a coat. Instead, he has to wear the same old hoodie 24/7."

"Well, at least he isn't wearing shorts."

"True, I had to draw the line somewhere. I'm sure the other moms are looking at him and judging me for what he has on. Or rather, for what he doesn't.''

Cash shakes his head. "I doubt it. Anyone who's ever been a parent knows exactly how stubborn kids are and that sometimes you need to choose your battles. And if they haven't learned that yet, they will. Sometimes kids are just assholes.''

I turn to face him with a smile. "Cash Hartwell, how did you become so smart when it comes to kids?''

He shrugs. "I may not have any of my own, but thanks to this town and Mom volunteering me at church for everything she can, I have had my fair share of mentoring. Would you believe that every fall I spend a day at the church helping with an adulting class? We teach all the incoming sophomores the basics of being a grown-up. They cover everything from changing a tire and checking oil to making a grilled cheese sandwich. It's actually a lot of fun and something I look forward to every year.''

I smile just at the thought of Cash instructing a group of young kids on how to change a tire. "I love that. Cash, you continuously amaze me with how much you love and support this town. We have so much catching up to do.''

"Well, Rae, as far as I'm concerned, we have the rest of our lives to get all caught up.''

I nod, blinking back tears building in my eyes.

Cash spies the moisture immediately and runs the back of his gloved hand across my cheek. "Hey, don't cry.''

I smirk. "I'm not sad, if that helps.''

He chuckles. "I know that. I just don't want your eyes to get frozen shut; it's too cold out here. If you cry and you blink, your eyelashes might stick together.''

I let out a loud laugh and playfully smack his arm. "You're ridiculous,'' I tell him as tiny snowflakes fall from the sky, adding to the magic of the parade.

"I've missed you." He admits. "I missed us."

I lean into him, resting my head on his chest. "I can't explain how good it feels to come back here. It's like this place has been a missing piece of me for years."

Cash wraps an arm around me and pulls me close. "You don't need to explain it, Rae. Because I feel it, too."

I snuggle in close to Cash as a Fawn Creek Police Cruiser begins to make its way downtown, with lights on and sirens blaring to start the parade.

Just then, Nolan turns to look at me, and I wave for him to come over.

"Sup?" He asks as he comes to a halt in front of us.

I furrow my brow. "Sup, I guess? Nolan, this is Cash." I motion to the man who is still standing with his arm draped around me.

Cash moves his arm and extends it to offer Nolan a handshake. "Hey. Nice to meet you."

Nolan shakes his hand and tilts his head to examine the stranger closer. "Did you bring your motorcycle?"

Cash lets out a laugh before exchanging a look with me. "No, I sure didn't."

"Why not?"

"I don't drive it when it's snowing."

"It wasn't snowing when you got here."

"Well, I checked the forecast before I left the house."

Nolan nods. "Makes sense. Can I drive it?"

Cash raises an eyebrow. "Do you have a valid Class M motorcycle license?"

Nolan pauses as though he's trying to understand the question. "No."

"Then my hands are tied, kid," Cash shrugs. "The last thing

I need is for you to wreck my bike without a valid license. My insurance would go through the roof."

"Not even once around the block?"

Cash shakes his head. "Afraid not. According to statistics, 89% of motorcycle accidents occur within three miles of the home. And Fawn Creek isn't even three miles wide, sooooo."

Nolan raises a brow. "Is that a true statistic?"

Cash shrugs. "Probably."

"Okay, you two." I step in, interrupting their exchange. "Let's actually watch the parade. Maisie will be coming by on the church float any minute, and then hopefully I can get her back here in time to see Sadie walk by with the band."

"Hey, I bet my mom will walk her down here so you don't have to miss seeing Sadie. Want me to check?" Cash asks.

I frown. While I'd love for Sharon to do that, I also don't want to take advantage of her. "That feels like I'm asking too much."

Cash laughs. "Reagan, with my mom you could never ask for too much. She loves you, and she has taken quite a liking to Maisie, too. She tells me I'm going to love her."

I nod. "You will. It's hard not to. She's a great kid. All of my kids are. Even the mad scientist over here." I motion towards Nolan who has rejoined his friends several feet away.

Cash fires off a text to his mom, and within seconds gets a response. "She said she will walk Maisie down here to us after she gets off the float. They are float number four, so Maisie shouldn't have to miss too much of the parade."

I let out a relieved sigh. "Good. I was worried that I'd have to rely on Nolan to catch candy for her. Last time he only saved her the Tootsie Rolls and peppermints. The bag he handed her looked like the bottom of my grandma's purse."

Within minutes, an old farm pickup with a banner on the front grille reading *Fawn Creek United Methodist Church Youth Group* makes its way down Main Street. Inside the truck, Pastor DeWitt and his wife, Linda, sit on opposite sides of the cab, tossing handfuls of candy to the children standing at the curb with their plastic bags at the ready. We wave to them, and survey the trailer attached to the back of the truck, holding a real-life nativity scene. Children from all over Fawn Creek are in costume as Mary, Joseph, the Wise Men, townspeople, and angels. My own angel, Maisie, breaks character for just a moment to scream, "Hi Mommy!" and wave her hand frantically in the air, as though I could miss her.

I wave back and take her photo just as she gets back into character, waving to the crowd and flapping her arms in front of her oversized angel wings.

I turn to look at Cash. "Did you volunteer to build that float, too?"

"I believe the phrase is, voluntold. I was voluntold to build the float."

I shake my head with a laugh. "You did a great job. I'm sure I could find you some things to do around my place too if you ever run out of church tasks."

He laughs. "I'll never run out of church tasks, but yes, I'd still be happy to. Say the word, and I'm there."

I grin. "Be careful. I might have more for you to deal with than you bargained for."

"Oh, I'm ready for anything." He replies with a smirk.

Before I can respond, the sound of the high school marching band interrupts our conversation. "Oh hey, here comes Sadie. She said she would be on this side of the street and in the third to last row. She plays the trumpet."

Cash smirks. "A trumpet, huh? That's what I used to play."

"Oh yeah, I totally forgot about that. She's loving band. She enjoyed it in Houston, but she seems to have really found her groove with this smaller school." I tell him while holding up my phone to get a video of her playing. "Maybe you guys can have a trumpet jam session sometime," I tease.

"Is that her, the one with the curly hair?" Cash asks, pointing.

"Yep, that's my girl."

"Interesting," Cash mutters. "Very interesting."

* * *

"Thanks for walking us home." I say, turning to Cash as we cross the old brick road and step into our front yard.

"Sure. I was happy to do it." Cash says, although his voice is rigid, almost as though he doesn't really mean it. "It was nice meeting you guys." He tells the kids.

"Nice meeting you, too." Sadie replies, causing her siblings to echo the same.

"Well, why don't you guys head up to bed and start working through showers?" I tell them. "School tomorrow."

"Maybe if we don't get a snow day." Maisie interjects.

"Oh, kiddo. I doubt you'll get a day off, but cross your fingers anyway. I'll be up in a bit to tuck you in."

The kids tell Cash goodbye and make their way into the house, leaving the two of us to stand alone in the gently falling snow.

I reach out to take his hand, squeezing it in mine. "I think that went well, don't you? The kids seem to like you."

Cash nods, taking a step back from me, his heavy boots crunching the snow beneath him. He releases himself from my grip. "Reagan. When were you going to tell me?"

I furrow my brows, and lean in to try to read his expression. It's clear that he's angry, but why? "Tell you what?"

"When were you going to tell me I had a daughter?"

Chapter 9

"Cash, wait!" I call out as I quicken my steps in an attempt to catch up with him as he storms away from me.

"Wait for what, Reagan? So you can lie to my face again?" Cash asks, turning on his heel to face me. Even in the darkness, I can tell that his face is glowing red with anger.

"I didn't lie to you!"

"Omission is still lying. And not telling me I had a kid for the last seventeen years? That's a massive omission!"

I shake my head, glancing back at my house and then back at him. "Cash..."

He takes a deep breath. "Do you have any idea how many nights I laid awake wondering what we might have been? And all this time we had a daughter together? Are you kidding me?"

I rest my hands on my hips and stare him down. "What are you talking about? Sadie is not yours."

Cash steps closer, pointing to the house. "Have you seen that kid? She has my nose and my eyes. She has Cassidy's curly hair. Hell, she even plays the trumpet like I did as a kid. Don't tell me you don't see it too."

"That could all be completely coincidental!" I argue.

Cash isn't buying it. "Oh sure. Total coincidence. Her birthday was last weekend! Do the math."

I shake my head. "Cash."

"That's almost exactly 9 months after you slept with me over Spring Break and then disappeared. Did it seriously never cross your mind to tell me? Or were you just hiding her from me? Maybe you aren't who I thought you were."

I shake my head. "Cash. We used protection."

"Condoms fail, Reagan! Isn't that the first thing they taught us in health class?" He throws his hands up into the air in exasperation. "As soon as you found out you were pregnant, you should have called me."

"It wasn't that simple. Mark proposed to me after I got back to school, and he asked me to move to Houston with him."

"You should have said no. You didn't love him. And you knew it, or you wouldn't have been with me while you were here."

"I thought I did. He promised to give me this incredible life if I just went with him, so I did."

"Yeah, well, how'd that work out for you?" Cash snarls, his words cutting through me like a knife.

"Not great, thanks," I frown, crossing my arms in front of my chest. Tears are streaming down my face. "That was a low blow."

Cash shakes his head. "Well, it's still not as low as hiding my kid from me, so I think I owed you one."

"Cash, you can assume that she's yours all you want, but you weren't the only one I was with. I was dating Mark before I came home. I slept with him plenty of times before my visit home over spring break, and plenty of times after, too. Just because you want her to be yours doesn't mean she is."

"Reagan, when you found out you were pregnant, you should have told us both. You should have given me the chance to order a paternity test instead of making the choice all on your own."

"I chose the one I knew was ready. I chose the one I was engaged to, and who I was sharing a bed with every weekend. I chose the one I assumed was the father."

Cash points a finger at me. "You chose wrong, Reagan. You can't look at that kid and tell me she isn't mine. I want a paternity test."

I throw up my hands in disbelief. "Oh, so you want me to just go ask my teenage daughter for a saliva sample so I can find out who her dad is?"

His jaw tightens. "Yes. That's exactly what I want."

I stare at him, my throat tightening with a mixture of anger and exhaustion. "It's not that easy. There's a lot at stake here."

He scoffs. "You missed taking the easy road a long time ago. I can't live in the same town as that kid for the rest of my life, wondering if she's mine. I want the test done, Reagan. If you don't do it now, I'll wait until she's eighteen and do it myself. It's going to be hell waiting for a year, watching her walk around, and not knowing for sure. But I will find out the truth eventually. With or without you."

I let out a haggard breath, the weight of it all pressing against my ribs. For seventeen years, I've ignored this possibility. Every time I saw a glimmer of Cash in her, I told myself I was wrong. I convinced myself it was impossible, and I was doing what was in her best interest. But maybe the entire time I was being selfish, and only really protecting myself.

"Fine, I'll do it." I finally decide, dropping my hands to my sides in defeat.

Just then, my porch lights up, causing a beam of light to spill into the street. We both look up to find Sadie standing in the doorway watching us. Her crazy curls, just like Cassidy's, fall over the shoulders of her red flannel Christmas pajamas.

"Mom, are you okay? Why are you yelling?" Sadie asks, concern dripping from her voice.

I wave in her direction. "I'm okay. Be right there." I turn back to Cash. "Perfect, I guess I'll go explain to my daughter that her life may have just completely turned upside down."

"Well, she's not the only one." He grumbles before turning to walk away.

I watch for a second as he makes his way back towards Main Street before turning back to Sadie. "Okay, kiddo. We need to talk."

* * *

Sadie picks up a throw pillow from her bed and places it in her lap, smoothing her fingers over the embroidered stitching. It's almost as though she is aching for something tangible to concentrate on as she digests what I just told her. "So, what you're saying is that Dad might not be my dad after all?"

I gulp, the words catching like gravel in my throat. "I know it's a lot to take in. And the truth is, I can't say for sure. It could be Cash. Or maybe it's Mark. The test is the only way to know for sure."

She nods slowly, still staring at the pillow. "And you've just been hiding this from me?"

"No," I say, reaching out to gently touch her arm. "Sadie, I swear I really believed that Mark was your dad. I would have never kept something like this from you."

"So, what happens now? How do we find out?"

I shrug. "We take the paternity test and then we will know for sure. I will need to call the clinic and see what we need to do."

Sadie nods before slowly moving to meet my gaze. Her eyes search mine for answers to questions that I don't know how to answer.

"I know this is a lot, Sadie. I'm so sorry. Are you okay?"

She pauses for a beat before answering. "I think so. Can you call the clinic tomorrow?"

I nod. "As soon as they open. I promise."

* * *

"Okay," Dr. Christensen says as he turns to the sink to wash his hands. "We will get these samples sent off to the lab for you."

I nod, exchanging a look with Sadie. "Has Cash already been in?"

He nods. "Yes, he stopped by this morning as soon as we opened, and we got his sample. We should have your results back in two to five business days."

"Perfect," I mutter under my breath, attempting to calm my shaking voice. *Two to five business days.* By this time next week, we will have answers. By this time next week, we will know if Sadie has a completely different family than she was raised to know. I feel ill.

Sadie and I make our way out of the downtown doctor's clinic and onto the sidewalk. "I don't suppose I could talk you into a latte before you take me back to school?" Sadie asks with a half-smile. She knows me well enough to know that I never miss the chance for a caffeinated treat, no matter the time of day. Especially while I'm already drowning in guilt over what we just did.

"Oh sweet child, you can always talk me into coffee." I remind her, squeezing her hand. "Are you okay?"

"Yeah, it's a lot," she admits, "but I had a lot of time to think about it last night. Maybe this isn't a horrible thing. I mean, if Cash is my dad, that opens up a whole new family for me to get to know. Mark is going to freak out, though. Do you think he will disown me?"

I shake my head. "Of course not. Listen, your dad may not have been a great husband to me, but he has always been a good dad. Nothing could make him stop loving you."

She nods. "I guess you're right."

"I am. I remember the way Mark looked at you the day you were born, and I was so lucky that I got to watch firsthand when he met you and fell in love with you. Nothing will change that." I assure her. "He will probably be mad at me, but I'll worry about that. That's my mess to clean up, not yours."

"Cash seems like a pretty cool guy. He wouldn't be a terrible dad," Sadie says, as we continue our walk towards Drip. "And I've seen the way you look at him. You loved him, didn't you?"

Sadie's words cause me to pause for a beat. When did she become old enough to have this kind of grown conversation?

"Yeah. I did." I admit. However, I don't admit that I think I still might be in love with him after all these years. One big revelation at a time.

Sadie and I step into the coffee shop to find Cassidy standing at the counter.

"Hi ladies!" She greets us with a warm smile. "What can I get started for you today?"

"I'll have a medium peppermint mocha latte." I decide after briefly reading a chalkboard sign showcasing all of Drip's seasonal drink specials.

"Medium dirty vanilla chai latte for me." Sadie adds.

"Both hot?" Cassidy confirms.

"Please." Sadie and I answer in unison.

"Coming right up," Cassidy answers as she moves to fire up the espresso machine. "So, what are you ladies out doing this morning?"

Sadie and I exchange a glance.

"Oh, just a doctor's appointment." I answer vaguely. I know Cash is Cassidy's nephew, but who knows what he's relayed to her, if anything at all.

"Everything okay?" She asks, with obvious concern on her face.

"Yes!" I answer, probably too quickly. "Just a routine appointment."

"Oh good. We can't have you getting sick this close to Snowball," Cassidy tells Sadie with a soft smile. "Especially with you being in the running for Snowball Queen. I saw a photo the school posted on Facebook of all the candidates."

I turn to Sadie, with an obvious look of confusion on my face. "What's Snowball? And why didn't you tell me you're in the running to be the queen?"

Sadie shrugs. "Snowball is the winter formal at school the weekend before Christmas. And I didn't tell you I was in line to be the queen because it's stupid. It's not like I'm going to win. It's just a popularity contest."

I scoff. "And why wouldn't you win? Obviously you stand a chance if you were chosen as one of the candidates."

Sadie rolls her eyes. "They probably only chose me because they feel sorry for me since I'm new. Now, I have to go to the dance and stand in front of everyone in a stupid dress so that someone else can be chosen and I can feel like a loser. It's dumb. They should at least let people decide if they want to be a candidate in the first place."

"Snowball is a lot of fun. My daughter, Sierra, always had the best time when she went." Cassidy interjects, sliding our drinks across the counter to us.

I hand her my debit card before turning back to my daughter. "Sadie, I think you should go."

"Oh, I don't have a choice." Sadie groans. "But that means I have to find a dress, and someone to tame all of this," Sadie says, motioning towards her hair.

Cassidy perks up. "If it helps, my daughter is actually a cosmetologist here in town. She has her own salon. Why don't I give you her card? I'm sure she'd love to help with hair and makeup if you need it. She's a curly-haired girl too, and she knows how to work magic with it." She slides the card, as well as my debit card, across the counter to us.

"Thank you." I offer her a soft smile as I tuck the cards into my wallet. "Okay, well, we better get this girl back to school."

"Okay, have a good day. Oh, also, the thrift store here in town almost always has some great dresses for cheap if you don't want anything over the top."

"Oh, that's a good idea." Sadie says excitedly before turning to face me. "Can we go look? It's just right there."

"You really need to get back to school." I remind her.

"I'm not missing anything special. By the time I get back to school, it'll be ten minutes until lunch. Please?"

I roll my eyes, but ultimately I can't turn down a reason to dress shop with my oldest daughter. "Fine. Let's go see what they've got."

Within twenty minutes, Sadie and I are making our way out of *Next*, Fawn Creek's adorable little thrift store, with a bag full of things we didn't know we were looking for.

I shake my head. "I can't believe you not only found a snowball dress but also shoes for under twenty dollars. Leave it to my daughter to find Converse to match her formal dress."

Sadie laughs. "If I'm going to have to wear a dress, I might as well at least wear comfortable shoes. Besides, I am too clumsy for heels. If I break my ankle at Snowball, I'll be walking in a boot over Christmas break. I wish that the Letterman jacket in there had fit me, though." She adds, reminding me of the jacket hanging on the back wall. She squealed and ran to it when she saw it. Unfortunately, it was a size 2X and completely swallowed her tiny frame.

I frown. "Yeah. I know, kid. I'd love to say that I could order you a new one for Christmas, but it wouldn't be back in time."

Sadie shakes her head. "No way. New Letterman jackets are expensive, and I just really like the vintage look of the one that was at the thrift store. Maybe I'll find another one, one day. At a garage sale or something."

I place my hand on my chest to appear shocked. "Vintage? Really? That was the exact one that the boys in my graduating class wore in high school. I don't think I'd quite call it vintage."

Sadie shrugs. "Well, you did graduate like twenty years ago, so..."

"So, you're calling me an antique? After I bought you coffee and took you shopping during a school day?" I place my hand on my chest for dramatic effect. "How dare you?"

"Hey, it's a compliment. I love vintage stuff." Sadie smirks, trying to recover. It's not working.

I roll my eyes. "Girl, get in the car. I have to take you back to school and then order myself some eye cream."

Chapter 10

"Okay, give your lashes a quick coat of mascara and then you are ready to roll out, girlfriend." Sierra says with a wink as she steps back to admire a job well done on Sadie's hair and makeup. "Be right back." She adds before disappearing into the back room.

"Sadie, you look incredible." I gush. "Way too grown up, but incredible."

Sadie may have walked into Fringe as a shy 17-year-old girl who lacked confidence, but that girl is no more. Instead, in front of me is a beautiful, confident young woman. And you can tell by the way she continues to admire herself in the mirror that she sees it, too.

"Well, Mom, don't forget this is my last year as a child. I will be an adult in less than a year." Sadie reminds me.

I frown. "Ma'am, you've only been seventeen for a couple of weeks; there is no need to rush things."

Sadie screws the lid back on her mascara and places it on the vanity in front of her before climbing out of the salon chair and standing to admire herself in the full-length mirror. "I can not wait to get home and put on my dress."

I smirk, happy to hear a change in her outlook about the night. "Well, you sound excited to go tonight at least. What changed your mind?"

"Honestly? Sierra. She made me look so good, and the way she just hyped me up the entire time she was doing my hair and makeup didn't hurt either."

"Girl, you deserve to be hyped up." Sierra says, returning to the room. "You are stunning."

"Well, the magical products you used on my hair sure didn't hurt either. I can't believe how great my curls look."

"Your hair is beautiful. You just needed the right tools to truly make them shine." She says, handing me a small plastic bag. "Here are some samples of what I used on your hair tonight. If you like them, I can order you a full-size set. No pressure, though. Good products aren't cheap."

"Sold," I say, not giving Sadie the chance to respond. "That sounds like a great Christmas gift she can actually use."

Sierra smiles. "I'll get some stuff ordered for you and let you know when it comes in. Send me a picture of Sadie in her dress, too. I need to see the final product once everything comes together."

I hand Sierra cash to pay for her hair and makeup service and thank her, just as my phone vibrates in my pocket. I pull it out to check it as Sadie works to put on her coat and gather her things.

It's an email from the Fawn Creek Health Clinic.

The results are in.

Quickly, I log into the database and scan over the text.

Fawn Creek Health Clinic
 Paternity Test Results Available
 Probability of paternity: 99.999%
 Conclusion: The tested male can not be excluded as the biological father.

My stomach drops. There it is, in black and white. No more guessing. No more what if's. Just the truth staring back at me after all these years.

Cash is Sadie's father.

"Mom, what's wrong?" My daughter asks, breaking my concentration and snapping me back to reality.

I shake my head and slide my phone back into my jeans pocket. "Nothing. Sorry. Let's go home and finish getting you ready for your dance."

* * *

"I can't believe you signed up to be a chaperone." Sadie says, closing the car door as we climb out of my SUV in the high school parking lot.

"In my defense, I really didn't have much of a choice. The drama club teacher cornered me while I was subbing last week." I admit closing the car door and joining her to walk towards the building. "She practically made it sound like the dance would be canceled if I didn't agree to help."

"You couldn't have lied? Said you didn't have a sitter? Made up some other excuse for not being able to make it?"

"Am I that embarrassing to be seen with?"

"No, it's not that. It's just that I feel like I have a magnifying glass on myself already. I'm the girl with the hot teacher mom. Now, my hot mom is going to be at the dance in a sexy tight black dress? You know I love you, and I'm all for body positivity, but the guys in my math class are going to be annoying as hell on Monday. As if they weren't already."

I pause on the sidewalk, looking down at my black knee-length dress. "This dress isn't sexy, is it?" I ask. "I made sure to wear something that reaches my knees and has sleeves. It's modest enough, right?"

"It's not the dress, Mom. It's the body." Sadie huffs.

Just as I open my mouth to argue, two girls make their way down the sidewalk towards us interrupts us. It's not long before I'm able to make out the faces of Becca and Courtney.

"Sadie!" Becca calls out as she speed walks towards us in a sequined royal blue cocktail dress. Courtney trails along beside her in a black velvet dress. "You look amazing."

"So do both of you!" Sadie answers, moving towards her friends and pulling them into a group hug.

Quickly, I snap a photo of their embrace with my phone, without them noticing, before instructing the girls to pose for a few more pictures.

"Okay, ladies, you are free to go. Sadie, I'll send these pictures to you now."

"Thanks, Mom."

"Thanks, Sadie's mom," the other two girls echo.

I pause, watching the girls make their way towards the school. Arms linked, giggling and whispering all the way down the sidewalk.

Seeing Sadie with her friends causes my body to flood with relief.

My baby is going to be just fine in this little town. Even after she finds out about Cash, at least she will have good friends to turn to once her world is rocked.

* * *

83

"Mom! I'm going to go with Becca and Courtney to Sonic, is that okay? Becca borrowed her mom's car, so she's driving."

I look from my daughter to her friends, who are standing behind her, waiting for my approval. My daughter was not crowned Snowball Queen tonight, because she's right; it is a bit of a popularity contest. However, she was so relieved not to be the center of attention. If the loss makes her happy, I'm just fine with it, too.

"Home by midnight." I tell her with a soft smile.

"I will be! Thank you." Sadie agrees with a smile before turning back to her friends and following them out of the gym.

"I think we are all done here, if you want to head out." Mrs. Blackart, the high school drama teacher, tells me as I finish wiping down the last table. "Thank you again so very much for helping tonight. I know chaperoning probably isn't how you wanted to spend your Friday night, but I appreciate you."

I wave her off. "It was actually a lot of fun to see the kids outside of the normal school day. I enjoyed helping. And it gave my younger two a reason to stay with my parents for the night."

"Well, enjoy your quiet evening then. Thanks again," she says with a wave as she turns to direct her husband to carry away the last remaining folding table.

After a short drive home, not even long enough for my car to fully heat up, I pull into my driveway and pause, taking in the stillness of the neighborhood. The porch light on my wraparound porch is lit up. Aside from that, the only light coming from my house is the soft glow from the white lights of our Christmas tree peeking through the front window. I can't quite explain it, but the sight of the lights puts me at ease. As though for the first time in a long time, I'm finally somewhere that feels like home.

I shut off my car and go inside, kicking off my heels in the entryway. Then, I make my way to the kitchen and pour a glass of wine before returning to the living room. I don't turn on any lights or the television; instead, I just sit in silence with my legs curled under me and a blanket over my lap as I enjoy the quiet.

That is, until I hear the familiar rumble of a motorcycle making its way down the street towards my house. I pause, waiting for the bike to approach the curb in front of my residence, and it does. Cash kills the engine and I brace myself, listening for his boots to clomp across the wooden porch. Even still, I jump just slightly when he knocks on the door.

I let out a heavy breath, slide my wine glass onto the table and then make my way to the door to let him in.

"Hi." I offer with an anxious smile.

"Hi." He replies softly. "I got the results."

"Yeah, me too." I nod.

"Does she know yet?" he asks quietly, leaning against the door frame, as he looks towards the staircase.

I shake my head. "No, she had her dance tonight. I didn't want anything to distract her from having fun. She's out with her friends right now."

Cash nods and then turns to look over his shoulder as though expecting to see Sadie standing behind him before turning back to me. "Reagan, look. I need to apologize. I know I overreacted when all of this came to light. And I shouldn't have acted the way I did or accused you of lying to me."

"It's okay." I assure him. "I mean, who's to say what the right response is in a moment like that?"

He shakes his head. "It's not okay to yell or accuse people. I know you're a good person. I've known your heart since you were a kid, and you wouldn't have just hidden her from me.

It just threw me for a loop," he winces. "You know, I always wanted kids. I thought you and I were going to have a houseful of them. Then, we broke up, and I assumed I'd find someone and settle down and have a family, but it never happened. I never loved someone enough to start a family. Not like I loved you." He looks deep into my eyes, and even in the darkness I can see a trace of tears building in his eyes.

I hurt him, and I hate myself for it.

"When I saw Sadie, it just broke me. I knew she was mine the second I saw her, and all I could think about was all the years I missed," Cash shakes his head, like he's trying to clear those same thoughts from his brain once more. "I hated knowing that she's been in this world for all this time and I'd missed everything because I didn't know."

"Cash, I'm sorry. I never meant for this to happen."

He nods. "I know. What do we do now?"

I frown. "I guess we wait for her to get home and we tell her together. Want to come in?"

Cash nods, accepting my invitation, and steps inside, kicking his boots off in the doorway.

I point to my glass of wine. "Want some?" I offer.

He scrunches his nose. "Wine? No thanks, I'm not quite that fancy. I'm more of a Busch Light kind of guy."

"Suit yourself." I say with a laugh before sitting back down on the sofa and covering my legs with my blanket. I let my one free hand rest in my lap while Cash and I fall into an awkward silence.

Cash finally speaks up. "Rae, I really am sorry," he whispers. "I wish I could go back in time and change how I reacted. I know that nothing you did was malicious, and you only had her best interest at heart for all these years."

Cash slips his hand into mine, and I squeeze his fingers tightly. "Cash, I promise you I truly did not know that Sadie was yours. You and I were careful. I made sure of that. So, I truly believed Mark was her dad."

He nods. "I get it. He probably was the better option at the time. I had some growing up to do."

I shake my head and take a sip of my wine, letting the sweet liquid run down my throat. "We both did. And in hindsight, now I wish I had questioned it. Maybe my life wouldn't be such a mess." I admit as I take a deep breath, hoping the wine will give me the courage to say what I need to say.

"Cash, that night happened for a reason. I knew Mark was going to propose, and I knew I was going to say yes. But also, I came home that Spring Break with one goal in mind; to get you out of my system. It's like when we thought we were cool as kids and picked up smoking cigarettes one summer. Yeah, we were pretty cool until we couldn't just quit. I just kept thinking that I just needed one more drag, and I'd never touch them again for the rest of my life. That night with you was my one more drag. I thought we'd sleep together, and I'd get you out of my head, and I'd be able to really say goodbye."

Cash lifts a brow to look at me. "Did it work?"

I roll my eyes. "What do you think? We couldn't be alone together in my kitchen for ten minutes before my tongue was down your throat."

Cash lets out a chuckle. "Well, you certainly didn't hear me complaining about that."

"Oh, I noticed."

Cash scoots in closer to me. "Reagan, I still really want to make this work. Me and you. Obviously, Sadie's feelings need to come first, and if she needs some time to wrap her head around us, then I'll give her the time she needs. But I want you to know that I will not let you run away this time. Not now that I have you back in my life and in my arms. I want to finish what we started when we were kids. I want to see how far we can take this."

Just then, before I can even respond, I hear the front door open and Sadie's Converse kick off into the pile of shoes that Cash and I started.

"Mom? What's going on?" Sadie asks, entering the room. Her expression makes it clear that she already knows the answer, but she asks anyway. "Did you get the test results?"

Cash and I exchange a look, yet don't release the grip on each other's hands.

"Sit down, sister. Let's have a chat."

Sadie takes a seat, barely perching on the other side of the sectional sofa. "So, it's true? Cash is my biological dad?"

I nod slowly, searching my daughter's eyes for any sign of how she's feeling. "Yes, it's true." I finally admit.

She nods. "Are you going to tell Dad... I mean, Mark?"

I hold up a hand. "Slow down. Mark is still your dad, too. Yes, I am going to tell him because that's the right thing to do, but I promise you that his love for you will not change."

"Think of me as more of a bonus dad," Cash offers nervously.

"My bonus biological father." Sadie says with a bit of a smirk.

"I know this is weird." I offer. "And Sadie. I'm sorry. This wasn't the plan, and not anything I ever wanted to put you through. But here we are. All we can do is move forward at this point."

"Are you two dating again?" Sadie asks, raising an eyebrow.

I shuffle uncomfortably in my seat, exchanging a glance with Cash before answering her. "Is that okay?"

Sadie snickers. "Is it okay that my mom and dad are dating? Yeah, it's a little weird, but fine. I don't hate the idea of having parents that actually like each other."

I let out a low chuckle before leaning across the sofa and squeezing her hand. "Really, kid, are you okay?"

She nods. "It's just a lot to take in, but yes, I am. It's good to have answers." She turns her head to look at Cash. "What do you want me to call you? Dad? Cash?"

He shrugs. "Whatever you're comfortable with. We don't have to rush into anything if you don't want to."

"When are we going to tell Nolan and Maisie?"

I look at Cash and frown. It hadn't even crossed my mind that I was going to have to explain this to my younger children. I look back at Sadie. "Whenever you're ready, I guess. Whatever you are most comfortable with."

Sadie smirks. "Nolan is going to be pissed that my dad has a motorcycle and his dad rides around in a golf cart at the club, driven by a caddy."

Cash and I lock eyes, both attempting to hide our laughter.

I think our girl is going to be okay after all.

Chapter 11

"Daddy's here!" Maisie calls up the stairs excitedly.

"Yay." I mutter under my breath, leaning over my vanity to put on another coat of mascara. I haven't seen Mark since the day we left Houston. The kids have talked to him, of course, and he's sent me texts about this visit, but seeing his face is a whole other ballgame. Plus, the fact that he's bringing Brittani? Ugh. It's going to be a long day.

The plan for today is that Mark and Brittani are going to go to church with us so they can see the play. Afterwards, we are going to come back here, where the kids will have Christmas with their dad and eat lunch. All I can hope is that I can stay hidden in the kitchen or upstairs for as much of it as possible.

Oh, and as an added bonus. I still need to tell Mark that Sadie isn't his biological child. *Surprise! You've been raising another man's child for the last seventeen years. Turns out Mark wasn't the only slimeball in this story.*

I slide on my boots and look at myself in the mirror once more before I walk downstairs. I'm wearing black leggings, a red tunic sweater and black booties. Today, I feel good, and I look good. I finally feel as though my life is really coming together in Fawn Creek. Now, I have to just face my old life and the mistakes I made that led to the very hard discussion I need to have today.

I take my time moving down the stairs, listening to the chatter from my youngest child and my ex-husband coming from the kitchen. I enter the room to find Maisie sitting at the table finishing her breakfast, and Mark sitting in a chair next to her, listening to her go on excitedly about the play. Brittani is standing in the corner of the kitchen with a bored expression on her face while she stares at her phone. She honestly looks like she wants to be here less than I want her to.

Time to kill them with kindness.

"Hi." I say to everyone in the room as I move towards the counter to refill my coffee cup.

Mark smiles brightly. "Reagan. Good morning. You look..." before Mark finishes his sentence, his eyes move to meet Brittani's. The akwkard silence in the room is deafening. She is staring back at him with a raised eyebrow. "Well." He finishes. "You look well."

"You too." I offer back. I hate to admit it, but he does. Guess all of that jogging around our old neighborhood has done the man some good health-wise.

"Maisie, are you about ready to go? I think they said you need to be there by 9:15 to get in costume." I ask in an attempt to redirect the uncomfortable conversation.

"I'm so ready!" Maisie says, flying out of her seat. "I think this is the most ready I've ever been for anything in my entire life."

I let out a soft snicker. "Okay, well, let's get going then. Sadie, Nolan! We need to go!" I call up the stairs to my older kids, causing a loud stampede of feet to make their way down the wooden staircase.

I stand back, allowing Mark to greet his other two children.

"Does anyone want to ride with us?" Mark offers as he pauses next to a massive pile of wrapped gifts that were not there when I went to bed last night.

I furrow my brow at the mountain of presents. "What's all this?" I ask, motioning towards them.

"Well, we're going to do gifts after church, right? I just figured it would be best to bring this stuff inside now. There are a few more things outside, but I'll explain that when we get back."

I frown. "What all did you.... No, never mind. We have to go." I shake my head.

"I'm riding with Dad!" Nolan pipes up.

"I'm riding with Mom," Maisie decides. "She knows where she's going."

"Sadie, what about you?" Mark asks our daughter.

Sadie looks up from her phone and bounces her eyes from me to Mark. "Mom." She replies quickly.

"What, you don't want to hang out with your old dad?" Mark teases.

Sadie looks directly at me and raises a brow as though sending me a secret message to interject.

I nod as a silent sign of understanding. "We'd better get going! Don't want to be late." I announce, opening the front door. "Let's go."

After getting Maisie situated in her Sunday School classroom to work on getting changed, I make my way out to the sanctuary. Lingering in the doorway, I pause to find my family, which doesn't take long at all. They are nearly taking up a full church pew.

Brittani is seated closest to the aisle, then Mark, Nolan, and Sadie. Sadie looks to be saving me a seat. After that slight opening in the row sits my mom and dad. This puts me almost as far from the center of the stage as I can get. Maisie made it very clear that I need to sit in the middle to be able to see her at all times. *That won't work.*

My eyes dart to the front row, where apparently the entire congregation is allergic to sitting. I can't blame them, after an unfortunate incident of Pastor DeWitt being accused of spitting on churchgoers during a very passionate service about the Sermon on the Mount. Even though this happened back when I was a kid, and no one can actually confirm if it's true or not, the people have not forgotten.

Well, come hell or high water... or even a little bit of spit... I'm going for it. It'll be worth it to see my girl in her first play and to see her face light up when she seems me in the crowd.

"Mom," Sadie hisses as she sees me take my seat. "I saved you a spot." She says, pointing next to her.

I shake my head. "I know, but I'm going to sit up here so I can see better. Come sit with me if you want to."

Sadie looks at Mark and then back at me. "I'm okay." She decides, obviously desperate to keep some space between herself and my ex-husband. I can't say I blame her. She knows part of the plan is to tell him today, and she is as anxious as I am about it.

Just as I relax in my seat, Cash makes his way down the aisle towards me, causing the butterflies in my stomach to go wild. And for once, it's not just because I'm falling hard for Cash Hartwell. This time, it's because my two baby daddies are going to be sitting within arm's length of one another. And one of them has no idea about the other.

"Hey," I say, as he takes a seat next to me. "I thought you'd get stuck backstage running lights or music or something." I tease. "Or maybe being an understudy for someone."

Cash snickers. "No, luckily I'm off duty for this performance, finally. I saw Maisie. She's pumped."

"Yeah, she is." I laugh. "She was up all night practicing her lines. I've truly never seen her so excited about anything ever."

"You might have a theater kid on your hands." Cash suggests with a shrug. "It could be pretty cool to watch her do that over the years. The high school kids have a Playmakers group, and they are actually a lot of fun to watch. I could see her dominating that in high school."

"Hi. I'm Mark." My ex-husband interrupts our conversation, sticking his hand between mine and Cash's shoulders.

Cash's eyes dart to mine before turning to shake his hand. "Cash. Nice to meet you."

"I'm Sadie, Nolan and Maisie's dad," Mark adds.

Oof.

I quickly jump in. "Cash, my ex-husband. Mark, this is my boyfriend, Cash." I say, introducing them to each other, while trying with everything in my soul to keep things light. Of course, all the while I'm praying that the show will start soon and we can move on.

"Nice to meet you." Cash says to Mark just as Pastor DeWitt walks on stage.

My prayers worked.

"Good morning!" The pastor calls out to the congregation.

"Morning." We reply.

"Ladies and gentlemen, today we have a very special treat for you. Our children's church has been working hard for the last few weeks to put together a production for us this Christmas. If what I saw at rehearsals was any indication, you are all in for quite a treat. So please sit back and enjoy *The Best Christmas Ever.*"

* * *

"Maisie, that was so good!" I tell my daughter, pulling her into a hug. "I am so proud of you."

"Great work." Cash adds, offering her a high five. "You're a star."

"Not going to lie, that was the best day of my life." Maisie tells us matter-of-factly. "I just want to be in plays for the rest of my life. Maybe the next one can be even longer than twenty minutes."

"Sounds good to me. I'll see if I can find you a local kids theater group." I say with a laugh, leading her back towards the rest of the family waiting for her outside. "We really enjoyed watching you. You're a natural, kiddo."

I step aside, joining Cash and allowing Maisie her moment with the rest of her adoring fans. Maisie makes her rounds, hugging her dad and her grandparents. Finally, she exchanges an awkward high five and selfie with Brittani before making her way back to me.

"Is it time to go home yet? Daddy says he got me the best present ever, and I want to go find out what it is."

Oh yeah, Mt. Saint Presents that's taken over my living room. I almost forgot.

"Yeah, let's go home and get to it." I tell Maisie before turning to Cash. "I'll text you afterwards? Wish me luck."

"Good luck. I can't wait to hear all about it," he says with a chuckle, but I know he's more interested in hearing about my chat with Mark than he is about the gift exchange.

"Bye, Cash!" Maisie calls to him as she runs towards my car to climb inside.

"Bye, Dad," Sadie says, almost as though she's trying it on for size, without realizing that she dropped a major bomb in the church parking lot.

Cash and I lock eyes. The younger kids do not know about the new revelation, so they don't even seem to notice.

Mark, however, did not miss Cash's new title.

I glance in Mark's direction to find him wide-mouthed, standing twenty feet away from me.

"Hurry up, guys!" Maisie calls out to me and Sadie from the backseat of my car through the open door.

I look at Sadie and send her a tight smile before leading her to the car, and leaving Mark perplexed on the sidewalk.

Chapter 12

"Okay, you guys are free to get started. I'm going to go get your lunch ready." I tell the crowd of people as they walk into my house.

Without a pause, I go straight into the kitchen, letting the swinging door close behind me. I'm already inside the fridge, pulling out the sandwich tray that I purchased from the grocery store yesterday when Mark joins me in the kitchen.

"Reagan, are you kidding me right now?"

I retrieve the tray and slide it onto the counter before turning to look at my ex, who is now visibly fuming.

"What? You don't eat sandwiches anymore? I expect that from your girlfriend, but not from you. I'm sure I can find a bag of almonds around here if she'd rather have that instead."

Mark's brow furrows. "This isn't about the food. Are the kids seriously already calling your new boyfriend, Dad? You two have not been dating long enough to start that already. That is so inappropriate, and frankly, I'm concerned."

I scoff. "Inappropriate? You want to talk about inappropriate? You brought your mistress to our family Christmas."

"Brittani is more than my mistress. She is my fiancée. We are getting married in Cancun the day after Christmas."

"Oh!" I exclaim, throwing my hands over my head. "And

that's why the kids couldn't come to see you for Christmas break. Because you'll be at an all-inclusive resort with a woman half your age. Got it."

"She is *not* half my age." Mark argues.

I roll my eyes. "Is she even old enough to rent a car?"

Mark leans in closer to me. "Stop trying to turn this around on me. At least Brittani and I have been together long enough to move on to the next step. Unlike you having our kids call your boyfriend dad."

Just then, Sadie sticks her head in the kitchen, interrupting our argument. "Um... you guys okay in here?" She asks with a concerned expression on her face.

I step back from Mark and turn to look at my daughter. "Yes. We're good. It'll be just another couple of minutes, okay?"

"Okay..." Sadie shrugs. "We can all hear you arguing, by the way. It's kind of embarrassing."

I frown. "Sorry. We'll be right out."

As Sadie disappears through the swinging door back into the living room, I point to the sliding patio door off the kitchen, indicating for Mark to follow me.

"Reagan, this is crazy. What are you trying to do? Turn the kids against me?" Mark asks as he steps onto the patio and I close the door.

"No, Mark, that is not the case at all." I say, shaking my head.

"Then what is it?"

I take a deep breath and tell him the truth. "Cash is Sadie's biological father." I confess, crossing my arms in front of my chest. "That's why she called him Dad. We just found out, and she was apparently trying out his new title without thinking of who could hear her."

Mark furrows his brow. "What are you talking about? You

got pregnant with Sadie when we were in college. We were practically living together."

I nod. "True."

Mark's face turns beet red. "So you cheated on me? When did you even have time to pull that off?"

I bite my lip. "Remember when you and your friends went on that graduation cruise? And I came home for Spring Break so I didn't have to be at school alone?"

Mark runs his hand through his hair. "So, you had an affair while I was on a guys' trip?"

I look at the ground. "Well, I wouldn't really call it an affair. It was very much a one-night thing." I admit. "I'm sorry."

"So, you had a one-night stand with a random guy almost eighteen years ago and you think he is actually Sadie's dad?"

"Well, I know he is. We did a paternity test, and he's the father. Also, he's not a random guy; he was my high school boyfriend."

Now the vein on Mark's forehead is poking out, a sign that he's really pissed. "Reagan, you seriously hid this from me for all these years? And then had the audacity to react the way you did when Brittani and I happened?"

I scoff. "Me sleeping with my ex-boyfriend one time before we got engaged was wrong, but you sleeping with your secretary after being married for sixteen years was way worse. Besides, I honestly didn't know she was his. I guess I always knew it was possible, but I never investigated it. I truly believed Sadie was yours. Cash is the one that did the math and asked for the test after he met her."

Mark steps away from me, rubbing his jaw and looking out across the backyard. "This is unbelievable. So, now what?"

"I... I don't know. I've never had this problem before."

"Sadie's still my daughter. Biological or not. I raised her, and

99

I love her, and nothing will change that." Mark demands.

I nod. "I agree, and Cash does, too. He just wants to be a part of her life, and she wants him to be."

Mark shakes his head, but doesn't respond.

"Listen, I know it's a lot to wrap your head around. And you have every right to be mad. But I truly believe there's no such thing as having too many people who love your kid. I think it's going to be okay."

"I guess it has to be, doesn't it?"

* * *

"Okay, sorry about that, everyone." I say, walking into the dining room with a tray of sandwiches. Carefully, I place them on the table and turn to my family. I pause to send Sadie a wink of reassurance before continuing. "I don't want to interrupt. You guys do your thing. I'll get your food set out over here, and you can graze as you want to."

"Yay! Finally, presents!" Maisie yells, jumping up and down on the couch cushion. "Mommy, stay and watch!" She demands before turning to Mark. "Can I go first?"

"No," Mark says, shaking his head. "You know the rules. Oldest to youngest."

I roll my eyes as I take a seat on a dining chair, just outside of their family gathering. This is one of the dumbest rules that Mark's family ever imposed on ours. What sense does it make to force the youngest, and definitely most excited, kid to go last at gift exchanges? It doesn't matter though; Mark has lived by this rule as if his life depends on it for years.

"Here you go, Sadie," Mark says after picking up a gift bag from the mountain of presents. He hands her the bag, and for a second they share a look. I wish I could read both of their minds.

As Sadie takes the bag, Mark lets his hand rest on Brittani's knee.

"I picked it out. I hope you like it," Brittani tells Sadie with an excited smile.

"Brit says that's what all the cool girls are wearing right now."

Sadie furrows a brow and digs into the bag, removing the tissue paper.

"It's a complete Lululemon set." Brittani explains excitedly. "It's a pullover, leggings and a fanny pack. And I got hot pink because I think that it is so your color."

I cringe for my daughter. Sadie is the last girl in the world who's interested in trendy things. She loves thrift stores and old records and the color black. I couldn't even get her to wear pink when she was eight.

"Thanks," Sadie says politely, stuffing the items back in the bag and gently placing the bag on the floor beside her.

Those clothes will never see the light of day.

"There's a receipt in there, just in case you want a different color or size." Brittani adds, pointing to the bag.

"And I threw a Starbucks card, plus a little extra cash in the bottom of the bag," Mark adds. "I wanted to make sure I spent about the same on each of you."

I turn to Sadie and wink. Looks like we are going to be making a trip out of town over Christmas break to return her gifts and get some more cash for her to go thrift store shopping instead.

"My turn!" Nolan exclaims, jumping up from his seat.

Mark walks over to the present pile and pulls out a large box. In seconds, Nolan has the paper shredded open. "A PS5! This is awesome. Especially since I'm still grounded from my PS4."

Mark turns to look at me. "He's still grounded? Really? It was a harmless prank."

I raise a brow. "He flooded the school, Mark. Yes, he's still grounded. I was planning to give him his controller back tomorrow, actually."

"Can I play it now?" Nolan begs. "Please?"

"Not until presents are done and your dad leaves." I tell him. "You need to spend time together while you can."

Nolan rolls his eyes and stands to gather food from the table begrudgingly.

"Finally, my turn!" Maisie exclaims, jumping up from the couch.

"Okay, you sit still." Mark commands. "I'll be back."

With that, Mark walks out the front door and returns with two plastic five-gallon buckets. He places them on the floor and invites Maisie to investigate.

Maisie meets him in the doorway and pries at the lid. "What's inside? Can I see?"

Mark opens the lid, and Maisie peeks in. "It looks like water." She decides.

"It is."

"You got me water for Christmas?" Maisie is perplexed.

"Well, that's just part of it. It's very special water that your Christmas gift needs." Mark says, picking up a box from the pile and handing it to Maisie. She opens the wrapping and the cardboard box, pulling out each individual item. Mark lists them off as she places them on the floor.

"A pump, a filter, plants, a log, rocks, test strips and worms."

"*Worms?*" Maisie squeals, making a disgusted face. "Why did you buy me worms?"

I exhale loudly. *Mark, what the hell did you do?*

"This one is next." Mark says, pushing a box towards Maisie, still not answering her. He's enjoying this a little too much.

She opens the wrapping to reveal a fish tank.

He got her a fish? Of all the things he could have bought her? A fish?

Everyone, besides Mark and Brittani, are perplexed at this point.

"Okay, one last gift." Mark says, opening the lid of a cardboard box and lifting a closed Tupperware container to hold in the air for Maisie to investigate.

"Is that..." I start, trying not to wring my ex-husband's neck.

"An axolotl!" Maisie squeals. "You got me an axolotl! What's its name? Is it a boy or a girl?"

Mark smiles proudly. "The name is up to you. You won't know if it's a boy or girl until it's probably eight months old."

"I'm going to call it a girl for now." Maisie nods. "And her name is Marshmallow. Mom, isn't this so cool?" Maisie asks excitedly.

"Very." I nod in agreement, sending a glare to Mark.

Leave it to my ex to get me more responsibility for Christmas.

* * *

"Cash! You have to come meet Marshmallow!" Maisie exclaims as she runs down the stairs just as I let Cash in through the front door.

"Marshmallow?" Cash asks, turning to look at me.

"My new axolotl. My dad bought it for me for Christmas."

"Like a stuffed animal?" He asks, raising a brow.

"No, it's real, and it's so cute."

"I didn't think those things were real. I thought they were like a Pokemon character or something." Cash mumbles to me.

"Oh, it's real all right. And I get to learn to keep its water properly balanced. It's the gift that keeps on giving." I mutter in response.

"Come see!" Maisie begs Cash once again.

"I'll be right there," Cash says. "Go wait for me."

"Okay, but hurry!" Maisie replies as she races back upstairs.

"I have something for Sadie," Cash confesses, as Maisie makes her way to her room. "It's my old Letterman jacket. I know you said she saw that one at the thrift store and it was too big. I think this one will fit. Honestly, if I can't pass it down to my daughter, who can I pass it down to? Is that weird? Is it too soon? Will she hate it?"

I shake my head. "No, she will love it. Let's go give it to her."

I lead Cash up the stairs to Sadie's room and knock on the door. "Hey kid, can we come in?"

Sadie, who is reading a book in bed, looks up from the pages to peer at us. "Sure. What's up?"

"I brought you a Christmas gift." Cash admits, taking a step towards her. "It might be stupid, and if you don't want it, it's fine. You won't hurt my feelings." He places the gift bag on the bed and takes a step back.

Sadie peeks in the bag and pulls out the jacket. "Is this the one from the thrift store?"

Cash shakes his head. "No, this one was mine. I figure it'll fit better than the other one would."

Sadie examines the stitches. "It's yours? You don't want it?"

He shrugs. "Not if you can get some use out of it. I can't think of anyone I'd rather have it."

She smiles. "And it has your last name on it. I love it. Thank you. This is the best gift I could have dreamed of."

Cash takes a deep breath. "You're welcome. Now, Sadie, I want you to know that I don't want to pressure you into any kind of relationship with me. I know you have a dad, and I know you love him. I don't want to replace him or compete. I just want to be in your life in any way that you'll let me."

Sadie nods. "Thank you. And I would like that."

Before Cash can speak again, Sadie jumps from her bed and gives him a hug, surprising the both of us.

"Thank you, really." Sadie says, standing back to look at him. "This means more to me than you will ever know. This makes me feel like you already know me."

"I can't wait to get to know you better." Cash smiles. "All of you." He adds, reaching out to squeeze my hand.

Epilogue

"Family and friends, it is my honor to present to you, the graduating class of 2026!" Principal Barton announces to the crowded gym.

Sadie and her classmates stand, throwing their caps into the air, just before the cans of silly string come out, playfully sprayed all over the gym among the graduating seniors.

"Man, for a class of 54 kids, they can sure make a lot of noise." Brittani says, hand resting on her growing belly.

I chuckle. "That's no lie. I'm glad the baby stayed put long enough for you to make it to graduation."

"Me too." Brittani smiles. "Missing this would have broken both of our hearts."

"Hi," Sadie says, making her way towards me, and pulling me into a hug. "Great job, Mom. I think you made it a whole thirteen minutes before you started crying."

"You were timing me?" I ask, brows furrowed.

"Maybe," Sadie laughs. "What else was I supposed to do while waiting to give my valedictorian speech? If I didn't find something to focus on, I was going to throw up on stage."

I shake my head. "I love you, kid. I'm so proud of you." I say, pulling her into a hug, fighting back tears once again.

"That was a great picture." Cash interrupts with a grin,

holding up his phone to show me the candid photo he snapped of Sadie and me mid embrace.

"I love it." I say with a smile. "Thank you."

"Mom, can you take one of me and Cash... and Dad, too?"

I nod. "Of course." I wait for everyone to get in place and snap the photo for her.

"Now one more, with you and Brittani too." Sadie says. "I want to make sure I have all of my parents together. It's not often that we have everyone together like this."

I can't help but pause for a beat before handing the phone over to my mom to take over. Sadie's always made me proud, but her growth since finding out about Cash and accepting everyone as part of her family amazes me.

Once the photos are done, Sadie excuses herself to run off to see her friends, and I relish one of the few quiet moments we will have today.

Cash smiles softly and pulls me close. "You okay?"

I nod. "Yeah. Today is just a lot... but so perfect."

"You did a great job getting her here." He says as he lifts my hand, kissing my knuckle just beyond my engagement ring.

"Watch out; that rock might poke your eye out." I tease. "I think you enjoy looking at my ring just as much as I do."

"It's true. The kids and I worked hard to pick that sucker out. Who can blame me?"

I smile softly. "Well, graduation is out of the way and we can breath for a little while. At least, until we start focusing on our wedding."

"And you will finally be Mrs. Hartwell. All those years ago, slow dancing with you at prom in this gym, I knew you'd be my wife one day... I just can't believe the road it took us to get here."

"Me neither." I admit. "But I'm so glad life brought me back here... and back to you."

About the Author

Michelle Lynn Ross is the author of humorous and heart-warming small-town romances set in Kansas, in the fictional town of Fawn Creek. When she's not writing, she enjoys traveling, reading, and spending time with her husband and three daughters.

You can connect with me on:

🌐 https://michellelynnross.com

📘 https://www.facebook.com/ThatsWhatShellSaid

🖊 https://www.instagram.com/michellelynnrosswrites

Subscribe to my newsletter:

✉ https://substack.com/@michellelynnross

Also by Michelle Lynn Ross

If you liked *Back to You* check out my other books set in Fawn Creek. These books are part of a interconnected series but can be read as standalone.

There's No Place Like Home

When Tyler Burris's long-term relationship falls apart, she's forced to return to her small hometown of Fawn Creek, Kansas—a place she swore she'd never live again. Her plan? Regroup, then get out fast. But between a rogue rooster, nosy neighbors, and a surprisingly charming (and grumpy) next-door neighbor, Tyler might just discover that what she's been searching for has been waiting for her all along.

Small Town Famous

After escaping a toxic relationship, Avery Thompson is focused on rebuilding her life and raising her daughter—solo. But when a new side hustle as a content creator brings unexpected attention (and chaos), she starts to find her spark again. Add in a swoony local cop who sees past her scars, and Avery must decide if she's ready to risk her heart... or let fear hold her back.

Single In A Small Town

After a messy divorce, Madison King is determined to start fresh—new hair, new walls, new life. The only rule? Absolutely no more Bryan Thompson. But in Fawn Creek, where dating options are scarce and secrets don't stay hidden, resisting temptation might be the hardest rule she's ever tried to keep.